*This collection of short stories is dedicated to my wife Jill
who waited patiently while I tapped away at the Laptop.
Thank you darling. XXX*

Contents

Bar Stool Preacher

I tended bar at Jimmy's. Corner of Washington and Cedar. Couple of blocks away from the big money places. Not that any of that money came into our bar. Wasn't that kinda place. It was mainly construction workers that drank at Jimmy's. We had a pool table, a juke box and a TV up high behind the bar. Apart from a few tables and chairs and a dozen bar stools, that was it. Nothing fancy. We didn't do food. No kitchen. We let the guys bring in their own stuff as long as they washed it down with our beer.

I came to Jimmy's in June, 98. I grew up in Boston. Never knew my Dad, he disappeared when I was four. Mum never spoke of him, so neither did I. No point. Why talk about something you've never had. Mum raised me best she could, but I was always a bit of a handful. I got in some scrapes and petty crime but nothing serious. When Mum passed in 96, I was nineteen. I took the eleven hundred dollar savings that she kept in the gravy tin, put a few things in a bag and left Boston to see the world. Eighteen months later I'd only got as far as New York.

I walked into Jimmy's Bar looking for work. He took me on there and then. Even let me have the backroom to sleep in. After a while he trusted me enough to run the bar on my own. After six months I rarely saw him at all. Maybe once every couple of weeks. The business was worth nothing, but the land it stood on was worth a fortune. Jimmy was just waiting for some developer to make him an offer he couldn't refuse. Till that day came, he left it to me to tend bar.

I opened when I wanted and I closed whenever the last person left. Then one day I met Mike.

Can I remember when?

You betcha. It was November 17th 1999. Why can I be so exact? Because it was the day after my twenty first birthday and I was nursing one mother of a hangover. The lunchtime trade had gone and the bar was empty. It was four in the afternoon. It would now be quiet until around five thirty when the same old faces would come in to have a few beers before heading home. There were times when some never made it and had to sleep it off in the back room. It was *THAT* kinda bar. I was clearing one of the tables and when I turned round he was there, sitting at the bar. I hadn't heard him come in which was strange as this guy was big. Six five and around two hundred and fifty pounds. He was wearing a black padded jacket, blue denim jeans and work boots. He had short dark hair with a few specks of grey. Difficult to say how old he was. Could have been any age from thirty to fifty. He had stubble on his face. Two days growth I'd say. I walked back behind the bar.

"Sorry, didn't hear you come in. What'll it be?"

He looked up at me and I know this is gonna sound weird, but he had kind eyes. See, I knew it would sound weird. But he did. Big... blue... eyes.

"Jamesons. Straight. No ice. Large."

I poured his drink and watched as he swirled it around in the glass. Staring at it all the time. Then he took a sip and sighed. I tried to make small talk.

"Haven't seen you in here before. You in construction?"

He looked at me as if he was trying to make sense of what I'd just said. Then he nodded.

"Oh yeah. Construction. Yeah, that's it. I'm in Construction."

After that I left him alone. He obviously wasn't the talkative type.

An hour later and the bar started to fill up. I better re-phrase that because I might be giving the wrong impression. It was a small bar. As soon as there were twenty guys in there it was full. They were all big guys, wearing big heavy clothes. So although it was filling up there were probably no more than a dozen guys.

I knew them all by name and I knew what they drank. So serving was easy. That's why there was only ever me behind the bar. I was in complete control. People came and went and by eight o'clock there were only four of us left. Me, Louis, Billy Mac and the new guy Mike.

Louis was reading aloud from a magazine.

"Hey, listen to this. It says here that seventy eight percent of Americans believe in Heaven."

I noticed Mike sit up and down his drink. He looked over at Louis.

"Statistics should be used the way a drunk uses a lamppost. For support not illumination."

He gestured for me to re-fill his glass.

It was the first words he'd said in almost four hours. But it was smart, clever and somehow profound. I liked it. I have to admit I didn't really understand it but I liked it.

By eleven there was just me and Mike. He'd drank best part of a bottle and a half of Jamesons but looked completely sober.

"What time do you close?"

I smiled.

"Whenever the last person leaves."

"Well I aint planning on going anywhere yet."

"In which case I aint planning to close up yet."

For the first time in seven hours I saw Mike smile. He left the bar at four in the morning. He'd sat on the same stool for twelve hours and drank two bottles of Jamesons. Yet walked out as sober as a judge.

Now you're probably wondering how I knew his name was Mike. Well, I didn't, but I was a skilled bar tender. Asking someone straight out what their name was could be seen as being intrusive, nosey and the kinda guys that came in this bar were the kinda guys that didn't like nosey people. So I used a technique that had never failed. Let's say some guy comes into the bar for the first time, he has a few beers then leaves. He comes in again a few days later, keeps himself to himself doesn't offer up any information. The third time he comes in. I begin to pour his drink before he gets to the bar. I then say.

"Hiya Davey, good to see you. Usual?"

I've just pulled a name from nowhere. He looks at me as if I'm mad.

"Who the fuck's Davey? My name is Bob!"

Bingo! I now know his name. I say something like.

"Sorry Bob. You look just like another one of my good looking regulars called Davey."

I give him his drink and then continue with something like.

"So Bob, hard day?"

Suddenly we're talking and he feels at home. I tried it with Mike. He didn't come in for three days then just like before he was there, outta nowhere. The first name that came into my head was Mike.

"Hiya Mike, didn't see you come in. Jamesons?"

He nodded.

"Yeah thanks."

I thought maybe he hadn't heard me call him Mike. So I did it again.

"Large, straight, with no ice. That's right Mike?"

"Yeah thanks."

What were the chance of that? Of all the names that I could have chosen I'd got his name right first time. Unbelievable!

He stayed until four again that night. Once again the last to leave. He paid his tab and then slipped me twenty bucks as a tip.

"That's for you for keeping the bar open."

Twenty bucks was a good tip back then.

"Thanks Mike. When you next back in?"

He shrugged his shoulders and left. He came back two days later. Same time, four o'clock, and sat at his regular bar stool.

"Hiya Mike. Good to see ya."

I poured him his Jamesons.

"Thanks."

George Bush was on TV giving a speech about American morals. Mike tipped the drink down his throat, sat up straight on his stool and took a deep breath. I knew he was about to say something. He did.

"I honestly believe that no one from Texas should ever be allowed to become President. One day people will think of that man as a joke."

There were six or seven people in the bar and it fell silent. Now there are two rules in a bar. Never discuss politics or religion. I waited for someone to speak up. No one did. Instead they all nodded in agreement.

Mike then continued.

"This man who insists that core moralism is what drives him will bring this nation to its lowest moral standing in history."

He pushed his glass forward and gestured for me to re-fill it. I did.

After that. Everyone called him the Bar Stool Preacher.

Mike became a regular over the next year or so. Three days a week. Usually Monday, Wednesday and Friday. You could set your watch by Mike. At one minute to four he wasn't there but sixty seconds later he was sitting at his usual stool sipping his first Jamesons of the day.

Yet, after all that time the only things I knew about him were his name and his profession. And, to be honest I kinda doubted both of them.

I began to notice certain things about him. He always wore the same clothes. Black padded jacket over a blue check shirt. Denim jeans and work boots. He always had two day stubble on his chin and his hair never grew. He never used the rest room. NEVER. He'd sit on the same stool for twelve hours drinking Jamesons and never once got up to take a leak or have a dump. How weird is that?

But he kept coming out with his profound statements.

One night Irish Dan was complaining that he never seemed to get a break in life. Good things always seemed to happen to other people. Mike sat up straight in his stool, knocked back his Jamesons and took a deep breath. The bar fell silent. We knew we were in for some of Mikes words of wisdom.

"If you do what you've always done, you'll get what you've always gotten."

Everyone nodded. The guy was right.

Usually by midnight it was just me and Mike in the bar. I'd be doing all the talking and he'd be doing all the listening. I'd try to engage him in conversation but the man was as tight as a clam. I was bored and decided to flick through the TV channels. I stopped when I came across some obscure cable channel showing back to back repeats of "I Love Lucy." It was one of my mom's favourite shows. Mike looked up and smiled as if he was remembering something from way back. I seized the opportunity.

"You like this Mike. You remember this from back in the day?"

He shrugged his shoulders and looked at me with those big baby blues.

"Maybe. Maybe."

Here's another strange thing about Mike. Everyone liked him. Now, no one knew him or anything about him. But everyone liked him. When the early evening crowd came in after work around five thirty the first person they said Hi to wasn't me. It was Mike. You'd hear things like. "Hi Mike" or "Hi Mikey" or "Evening Buddy". Everyone and I mean EVERYONE said hello to Mike. Mike never said Hi back. Just looked up and nodded. Guys would also buy him drinks. I'd serve them their beer and they'd say.

"Get one for Mike" or "Large Jamesons for my friend in the corner."

Once again he'd just look up and nod his head.

Three nights a week he'd stay till four in the morning. Pay his bar tab, slip me twenty bucks, then leave. But where did he go? Where the fuck did this guy live? Did he go straight to work or have breakfast somewhere? Was he married? Did he have kids? I'd known the guy for well over a year, spent hour after hour with him, considered him a friend, and yet I knew absolutely nothing about him.

Can I remember the last day I saw Mike? You kiddin me? How the fuck could I forget it?

But let's not get ahead of ourselves. For the best part of two years Me and Mike had our routine. He'd come in and sit on his usual stool. I'd serve him up his large Jamesons and he'd knock them back. When I noticed his glass was empty I'd fill it up. This would go on all night. Around midnight I'd stick on the cable channel and we'd watch "I Love Lucy" or sometimes episodes of "Bilco." I'd laugh out loud at these shows and if I was lucky

Mike might just crack a smile. At four in the morning he'd pay his tab, slip me twenty bucks, then leave.

Until the day everything changed.

It was a Monday and it was four o'clock. There was no Mike. At four thirty there was still no Mike. When the early evening crowd came in around five thirty there was still no sign of Mike.

The guys were concerned.

"Where the fuck is he? What if he's had some kinda accident or somin? We should call someone. The cops maybe?"

I could see how ridiculous that would be.

"And say what? That a guy who we think's called Mike and works maybe on a local Construction site. Hasn't turned up for his glass of Jamesons today. Anyone know where he lives?"

There was silence in the bar. Everyone shaking their heads.

"You see. Not one of us knows a goddam thing about him. So what chance do we have of finding out where he is?"

The atmosphere in the bar was strange that evening. No one really said much. One by one they left and by eleven thirty the bar was empty. I could have shut up for the night but I was hoping that maybe, just maybe Mike would turn up. Every Monday for almost two years I'd closed the doors of the bar at four in the morning. Tonight, with or without Mike, would be no exception.

The next few hours passed slower than a snail carrying a sack of concrete. Eventually with the clock showing just two minutes to four I opened up the till and started to cash up. I took out the notes, counted them and put them into a small brown envelope ready for banking later on in the day. I turned round.

"Jesus H Christ Mike, you scared the living crap out of me!"

There he was. Sitting on his usual stool, looking at me with those big blue eyes.

"Where the fuck you been Buddy, we've been worried sick aboutcha."

"He did what he always did. Shrugged his shoulders and sighed.

"Couldn't get away. But I'm here now. How about that Jamesons?"

"Yeah sure Mike. No problem. After the scare you gave me I think I'll join ya."

And then we did what we always did. I talked and Mike listened. But I noticed he kept looking at the clock on the wall. It was as if he was expecting something or someone. At seven forty five he stood up.

"Wanna join me for some breakfast?"

Wow this was a first. At last I'd get to find out where he went, maybe find out where he lived. Get to the bottom of this Bar Stool Preacher.

"Yeah sure Mike. Where?"

"Little place I know, not too far away. You'll like it."

"Okay. Let's go."

I locked the door and we stepped outside. Mike waived down a cab. He gave the driver fifty bucks.

"Brooklyn Bridge Park. Hurry."

"Really Mike, all that way just for breakfast?"

"Sure. You'll like it. Trust me."

The traffic wasn't too bad for that time of day. Most traffic was heading towards Manhattan and not away from it as we were. Mike spoke quietly.

"I won't be coming into the bar anymore kid. Time to move on. Been good to meet ya."

My heart sank. I didn't know him well but he felt like the closest friend I'd ever had. I struggled to find the words to say.

"That's too bad Mike. But never say never. Maybe come back sometime in the future?

"Maybe, maybe."

We were soon across Brooklyn Bridge and stopping at the park entrance. We walked into the park and stood on the pier looking across the river at the beautiful skyline of Lower Manhattan. It was a glorious morning. Mike kept looking at his watch.

"You okay Mike, you gotta go somewhere?"

"No, I'm fine just for a few more minutes. Like the view?"

"It's the best view ever, you wanna know why Mike?"

"Sure."

"Cos I know that at the bottom of those two magnificent Towers is a little bar that I call home."

Mike was standing behind me. I felt his hands on my shoulders.

"Listen to me very closely kid. Stay here. Do not go back. Understand?"

I turned round sharply to find out what the fuck he was talking about. But he was gone. In fact there was no one within fifty yards of me. I looked back at the skyline. It was 8.46 and a plane crashed into the North Tower.

So when people ask me if I can remember the last day I saw Mike. I say yeah, I can. It was the day that changed the world. By the end of that day, Tuesday 11th September 2001, Jimmys Bar was gone. Destroyed in a carpet of dust, concrete and debris.

Oh and by the way, did I mention about my Dad. The Dad I never knew, the Dad who disappeared when I was four?

His name was Michael….

Name In The Back Of His Clothes

Ronny Wells sat alone at the end of the bar. Not by choice, he'd have loved to have company, but he was the kind of man who didn't make friends easily. Apart from the barman he was sure that no one else on this shitty planet even knew his name.

He took a sip of his cheap scotch and smiled. He remembered something that a Sunday school teacher had once told him. "Write your name in the back of your clothes and God will always remember you." From that day on he did just that. Every piece of clothing he owned had RONNY WELLS written somewhere inside. It was on the labels on all his shirts, trousers and pants. Even his socks had RW written on the heels. He knew it was a complete load of bollocks but it had become a habit hard to break.

The pub was empty, well, apart from two low life's sitting in the corner, buying only lemonade and coke. A bottle of cheap scotch hidden in a Tesco bag under the table that they'd nicked from the off licence across the road. Terry, the barman knew what they were up to but turned a blind eye for a while. It was freezing outside and he knew they had nowhere to go. Eventually they became blatant and he told them to piss off. They didn't argue, they'd had warmth and shelter for two precious hours. Ronny held up his glass.

"Another large scotch please Tel."

The barman nodded.

"Coming up Ronny."

At least the barmen knew his name, unlike the almighty who had decided to have an away day for about twenty fucking years.

"Four sixty please Ron."

He handed the barmen a crumpled five pound note. It was his last.

"Keep the change."

The barman looked confused.

"You sure Ron?"

Ronny shrugged his shoulders.

"Yeh fuck it, why not."

Tonight was the night. No more pissing about. No more pretend. There was just nothing to look forward to. So tonight he would end what had become a miserable existence.

Why wait any longer? He was thirty six. No family on this god forsaken earth. His parents died when he was nine. Then a children's home, then foster parents who didn't give a shit and were only interested in how much money they got from the social. Then two years in a special unit for "wayward boys". Fucking joke that was. Then came prison.

Prison was a great escape. Three years in the scrubs were the best years of his life. He could hear other guys crying at night, what the fuck? It was the best time he'd ever had. Three good meals a day, clean clothes, a bed to sleep in, what more could you ask for.

He was lost when they let him out. Fucking lost. Big wide world, yet nobody to say hello to. That was fourteen years ago. He'd done a bit of work here and there. Some legit, some not. Didn't matter he survived.

But sitting there at the bar, he suddenly realised it was all a waste of time. So fuck it. Tonight was the night.

He sipped his scotch slowly. It was eight o'clock and the television in the bar was playing the theme tune to EastEnders. He smiled to himself. That would be the last music he ever heard. How fucking appropriate.

To get back to his squat he had to walk along the Thames and cross the old iron bridge.

He'd throw himself off. The tide and the cold would kill him in minutes. No problem. Job done. He would go to see his maker. Whoever the fuck that was.

"Night Terry."

The barmen nodded.

"Night Ronny, you take care now."

He walked out of the pub and along the old derelict pathway that led to the iron bridge. It was minus six and he shivered with the cold. What the fuck did it matter anyway. He'd be dead in a few minutes.

When he reached the bridge, he stopped and took a long look at the Thames. It was choppy and wild. It looked like it would swallow anyone up that challenged it. Fabulous. Why not. Life has fucked him and now he'd fuck life.

He climbed onto the steel railings and took a big gulp of freezing cold air.

"Ronny Wells?"

A voice came out of nowhere. He couldn't see anyone in the darkness. It spoke again. Only this time much, much louder.

"Ronny Wells?"

"Yeh? Who the fuck are you. How do you know my name?"

There was an eerie silence and for a few seconds everything seemed to stop moving. Even the Thames.

"Because it's written in the back of your clothes."

Lost In Acton

I'm an old man now. I'll be Eighty One in two weeks time. Still fit and healthy though. Walk to the shops everyday to get my shopping. Shoes polished, trousers pressed and always a clean shirt and tie. "Standards" as my old Mum used to say.

Mum was a stern lady. Some would say fierce. I only ever saw her cry twice and both times they were for my Dad.

I was born in 1936. I was just a baby when Dad went off to war. I remember him, but not sure if that's from actual contact or from photographs.

We had an old dining table in our front room. It had seen better days so Mum covered it with a big table cloth that touched the floor on all four sides. It became my play tent. I would get under that table and pretend I was in a magical cave.

And that's where I was in November 1943. Just seven years old when the man from the Army came to see Mum. I didn't hear all the conversation but I did hear him say "I am sorry to tell you that your husband has been lost in Acton."

That's when I heard Mum cry for the first time. It continued long after the Army man had left. I just sat in my tent not wanting to come out until Mum had stopped. It seemed like an age before I heard her stand up and walk into the Kitchen.

I was confused. Why was Mum so upset? We lived in Ealing and Acton was just a short bus ride away. If Dad had got himself lost then we should try to find him. Me and Mum had been there shopping loads of times. It didn't seem like a big place so finding Dad should be easy.

The next day was a Saturday so no school. I told Mum I was going out to play with Billy Jennings from across the road. I remember her words as I opened the front door "Don't go far and if you hear the sirens go off you come straight back. You hear me?"

"Yes Mum!"

Of course I had no intention of playing with Billy Jennings, the snotty nosed kid with the lazy eye from number forty six. I was going to find Dad.

When me and Mum went shopping in Acton the bus ride only took a couple of minutes so I knew it wasn't far. The number twelve Bus took one long straight road then dropped us at Acton Station. So all I had to do was follow that same road and I'd get there. I'd search the whole town and find Dad. I was certain of it.

It took half an hour. I walked some of it and ran the last few hundred yards. I saw the Station up ahead. I was in Acton.

I wandered around the town for hours. I looked in every shop, every store, every doorway and even every alleyway. But there was no sign of him.

Some shopkeepers asked me what I was doing. They obviously thought I was up to no good.

"Looking for my Dad!" I shouted, then ran as fast as I could into the next shop.

I was in the Butchers when I was aware of a large man in uniform standing in front of me. He reminded me of Dad. But it wasn't him. He looked down at me and smiled.

"So young man. What are you doing here on your own? Where's your Mum?"

"I'm looking for my Dad. He's got himself lost. Mum's indoors."

He took me to the Police Station and gave me a cup of hot Bovril.

"Now then son. You tell me what's going on."

So I did. I told him about the man from the Army coming to see Mum and how she started crying. I told him about what the man said about Dad being lost in Acton. He came over and put his arm around me.

"Let's get you home son. Your mum will be worried."

He put me in an old battered car and drove me home. When we got outside our house, he turned and looked at me.

"I'm going to speak with your Mum. Tell her what's happened. You sit there for a few minutes."

I watched as he walked up our path and knocked at the door. I saw him talking to Mum on the doorstep. Then Mum started to run towards the car. And that was the second time I saw her cry...

The Judas Calf

Patrick Burne stood in the study of the old house. The enormity of his task was beginning to sink in. The restoration work would take months to complete, and more importantly, tens of thousands of pounds. Money that he and his wife Laura had not entirely budgeted for.

They'd bought the house knowing that it needed a great deal of work, but they were young and positive and had high hopes of making this the sort of family home where they could raise their children.

It had previously been owned by an old Jewish man who had died with no family and had made no will. After months of correspondence with the Solicitor who was looking after the old man's estate, their offer had been accepted and eventually they completed the sale last week.

The house was sold to them exactly as it had been when the old man had died. It was furnished with old and not very valuable furniture. It even had food still left in the cupboards. It needed re-wiring, new plumbing, central heating, double glazing, a new kitchen and bathroom and a few walls knocking down here and there. Yep this would be a major project.

Patrick sat himself down at the old man's writing desk and started to rummage through the drawers. Mostly old receipts, but there was an old brown folder in the middle drawer. On the outside it had three words written on it. "The Judas Calf"

Patrick opened the folder and began to read.

My name is Joseph Weissman and I need to tell my story. I am an old man now and my time on this earth is coming to an end, but I must tell someone what happened during those terrible years.

It was a very long time ago and I was only twelve years old, but I can still remember the last day I saw my father.

The winter of 1943 was harsh. In our huts the temperature could be as low as minus twenty at night, and not get much warmer during the day. My two younger brothers slept with mother. All fully dressed and huddled together to keep warm. I slept cuddled up with father. We were allowed two blankets per family. So mother and the boys had one and father and I had the other. We were not alone in that hut. There were at least another twenty families like ours, all cramped together in a wooden hut no bigger than forty feet by twenty.

They called it Belzec.

We knew that there were two camps. The one where we and many more like us lived. Then there was the second camp. We were told that the other camp was the work camp, where things were much better.

Working meant food, food meant strength and strength meant life. The two camps were connected by a tunnel, or "tube" as my father would call it. Everyday hundreds would go through the tube to the second camp to work. But they never returned. Their place in our camp would be taken up by train loads of new arrivals.

There was a man in our hut called Demetri. He was friendly with the guards. His job was to take the chosen "workers" through the tube every day . He would tell them how great life would be once on the other side in Camp two. They would follow him. He would be laughing and singing and getting them to join in. But everyday he was the only one who came back. My father hated Demetri. I never knew why back then. He seemed like such a nice man. Then one day Demetri never came back. His place was taken by another man in a hut next to ours. He did and said the same things that Demetri had said.

Then one day he came into our hut very early. It was still dark outside. He had guards with him. He told all the men to get ready as they were being chosen to work in the other camp. My mother cried as she said goodbye to father. He kissed all of us and then got in line with the other men and made his way to the tube. I was happy for him. He would be working at last and being fed and getting stronger. I was sure that soon we would all be joining him. But I never did see him again.

Because father had gone one of our blankets was taken away. So every night all four of us would cuddle together under just one blanket to try to keep warm.

Two weeks later we were woken early by the guards. We were told that all the women had to leave to go to the work camp. I remember the screams. Some mothers had to be dragged away. My mother seemed to be resigned to her fate and smiled at me as she kissed us goodbye. I told her not to worry and that she would be with father and soon we would join her. She told me to look after my two younger brothers and not let any harm come to them. I told her that I would always protect them. She left and was gone.

There were more than sixty children in our hut. I was one of the oldest. I was very popular with the other children and would always try to make them laugh and do magic tricks that father had taught me. They trusted me.

One of the guards was called Karl. He would talk to me everyday. He would tell me how great things were in the other camp and how well mother and father were doing. He told me that we would all be reunited with our parents soon. He asked me to help him organise the other children. He said because they were so young and silly he would need someone like me to lead them through the tunnel. If I helped him with this he promised extra blankets and rations for me and my brothers. I agreed. It was cold and my two brothers were hungry.

The next morning I had all the children ready early. They were looking forward to seeing their parents again. When Karl arrived they were singing a song that I had taught them. The only children left in the hut were my two brothers. I followed Karl into the tunnel and we sung loudly. They were so excited, soon they would be back with their families.

After a very long walk in the dark and dimly lit tunnel, we arrived at the exit. There was a strange smell in the air, a sickening smell that I remembered from working for a short while in my uncle's abattoir. In front of us were large grey buildings with no windows but with a door at each end.

Karl told me to tell the children to run as fast as they could and enter the buildings. They are shower rooms he said, they must be nice and clean when they meet their parents. I told them to run. Run as fast as they could and get themselves clean. They ran. They entered the building and the guards closed the doors. Karl took me back through the tunnel. He said I had done an excellent job and he would need me to do it again from time to time. He promised that because I was being so good my mother and father would also be given extra rations and a much better place to sleep. I was happy.

I did this job for Karl about once a week from then on. My brothers and I were well fed and given new clothes and blankets. I could never understand why some of the older boys hated me so much. I was doing them a great service.

One day I took over three hundred children through the tunnel. All were singing and laughing eager to meet their parents once again. I was happy, I was doing a good thing.

When I returned that day my two brothers had gone. Karl told me that because I had done such an excellent job he had decided to re-unite them with mother and father. I was so happy I cried. Karl said it wouldn't be long before it was my turn.

But my turn never came. The camp closed the following year. I and three other boys were loaded onto a train and told we were going to another camp. Karl said our families were waiting there for us. We travelled for three days in a big carriage that smelt of urine and sweat. I heard a loud explosion and lots of gunfire. When the carriage door opened there was an English soldier standing there with his gun pointed at us. I thought he was going to shoot us all. Instead he gave us chocolate.

Eventually I ended up in England in a home for boys. I never knew the truth about my family until many years later and that's when it hit me. Hit me hard. Just what I'd done. Thousands of children had followed me. But please, please believe me. I never knew.

In abbatoirs they have something called a Judas Cow. It is the cow that leads the others into the slaughter house. It is the only one that survives. It does this job day after day. I pray to my god each day.

Please forgive this Judas Calf.

Patrick Burnes dropped the folder. Tears were streaming down his face. He was a Catholic. He also began to pray for The Judas Calf.

She Sees Dead People

"I see dead people."

I know what you're thinking. It's a good line from a good film. You'd be right. But the exact same words were said to me by an elderly lady by the name of Doreen Lucas.

Perhaps I'd better start at the beginning.

I'm a reporter on a local paper. The Rushbridge Gazette. Maybe "reporter" is a bit of a grand title.

Basically, people phone in or write to us about a local matter that they think worthy of our attention. I go round, find out more, decide whether it's true or not, then write a few hundred words for the paper. It's easy work. Usually it's about singing cats, talking dogs or maybe someone's grown a potato that looks like Prince Philip.

But a few months ago I got a call from a woman who said that her elderly neighbour had learnt Russian at the ripe old age of eighty six.

Seemed like a great local story so I set off to investigate. The only information I had was that the woman's name was Doreen Lucas and she lived at 58 Woodbridge Gardens.

The neighbourhood was classy. Big old Victorian houses, three storeys high and each with a large basement. Most had been converted into flats, but not number 58. This was still original. It would need a fair amount of TLC to restore it to its former glory but it was still a handsome house. The door knocker was a bulls head with a large brass ring through its nose. I knocked and waited.

An old silver haired lady, no more than five feet tall and not much more than seven stone stood in front of me with a smile as big as the house itself.

"Yes dear. What can I do for you? Have you come to read the meter?"

There was something about her eyes. Although she was looking straight at me, I couldn't help but think she was struggling to focus. Cataracts perhaps?

"No, Mrs Lucas. I'm from the Gazette. I wonder if you could spare me a few minutes to have a chat about you learning Russian recently."

She started to laugh.

"I bet it was that stupid woman next door who told you. Just because she heard me talking in the garden the other day. Come on in. I'll put the kettle on."

She turned and walked along the hallway leaving me standing on the doorstep. I wiped my feet and followed her into the kitchen at the end of the hall. There was a large wooden table and four chairs in the middle of the room. She patted one of the chairs as she walked by. I took that to mean I was to sit down. So I did.

"Tea? Milk and sugar?"

Before I could answer she quickly spoke again.

"Oh you take coffee. Black. I've got some in the cupboard somewhere."

She was right. I hate tea. Haven't had a cup in over twenty years. How would she know that?

"Yes please. If it isn't too much trouble Mrs Lucas."

She had her back to me and I could see her moving things about in a large walk in pantry.

"Can you help me? My eyes aren't what they were. I know I've got a jar in here somewhere but can't seem to find it. Don't want to give you a cup of gravy by mistake."

Once again she laughed. It was infectious. I started to laugh as well.

I walked over and found the coffee behind two cans of peaches and a tin of Ye Old Oak Ham.

"Here you go Mrs Lucas. Do you want me to make it?"

She took the coffee from my hand and unscrewed the lid.

"Don't be silly. You're a guest here. Go and sit down and I'll bring it over. And another thing. Stop calling me Mrs Lucas. It's Doreen."

I did as I was told and sat back down at the table. A few moments later she put a mug of hot coffee in front of me.

"There we go. Now what did you want to talk about? Oh yes. The Russian."

I took out a notebook and pen eager to take notes. I was now in interview mode.

"So you *DO* speak Russian then?"

"Well I wouldn't say I was fluent but I can hold a conversation."

"How did you learn it? Was it from your husband?"

Again she laughed.

"Reg? Oh no dear. Poor Reg was from Derby. Never left the country. Farthest he ever travelled was here to Rushbridge when we bought the house back in the fifties. He's been gone twenty years now."

"So how did you learn it? Books, tapes, classes?"

"Menya uchili russkiy yazyk menya khoroshiy drug Ivan."

I was impressed. The words were clear and precise. I had no idea if it was Russian or not but it sounded authentic.

"Was that Russian? What did you say?"

"I said I was taught Russian by my friend Ivan."

"Who's Ivan? A neighbour?"

"No dear. Ivan is a man who used to live in this house many years ago. He pops by from time to time. He taught me Russian so that we could have a chat together when he visits."

"That's nice of him. Does he still live close by?"

"No. He's long gone now."

"Did you and Reg buy the house from him?"

"No Ivan lived here a long time before that."

I was intrigued. What she was saying didn't seem to make any sense.

"When did Ivan live here?"

She sat back in her chair. Her head turned slightly away from me. I thought she was thinking. But she seemed to be whispering into thin air. Then she spoke.

"84."

Now I was really confused.

"But Doreen you said you've lived here since the 1950's. Was Ivan a lodger?"

She laughed that lovely laugh of hers then said the words that stunned me.

"No not 1984...1884!"

My first thoughts were simple. The woman was a nutter. But it didn't change the fact that she *COULD* speak Russian. Then she said something else that absolutely floored me.

"Your Aunty Dot says you've always been a nosey so and so."

She laughed as she said it.

This time I didn't laugh. My Aunt Dot had been dead for six years. She was my Mums sister and brought me up after Mum died. I loved her from the very marrow of my bones. When I was a kid growing up I wanted to be Clark Kent, Superman by night and a Newspaper reporter by day. She used to tease me and say. "You'll never be Superman but you'll make a good reporter you will, because you're a nosey little bastard."

I just sat there in shock. Doreen was smiling at me. The she said something else.

"Of course I'm being polite. She used other words."

I couldn't help it. I just blurted out.

"What words? What words did she use?"

Doreen stood up and put her hand on my shoulder.

"She said you were always a nosey little bastard."

She picked up the cups and walked away.

I sat there desperately trying to make sense of what she'd just said. How could she know? It was impossible.

Or was it? My rational mind took over. Rushbridge was only seven miles from where me and Aunt Dot had once lived. Maybe they knew each other. Maybe they were friends for a while. I stood up and walked over to her.

"Okay Doreen. You got me. You knew my Aunt Dot didn't you. Were you friends?"

She ushered me back to the kitchen table.

"Sit down and I'll get us both another coffee and we'll..."

She stopped in mid sentence as if listening to something.

"Better than that. Go to that cabinet over near the window. There's a bottle of something stronger in there. I'm told you like a drop of the hard stuff from time to time."

She laughed as she said it as though she was sharing a joke with someone unseen.

But she was right. I did like a drop of Whisky, sometimes a bit too much. I'd never been much of a beer drinker. Scotch was my tipple.

I went to the cabinet and found a bottle of Johnnie Walker Black label. Doreen was already sitting down at the table when I returned. There were two clean mugs on the table.

"I'll join you. But just a small one for me."

I poured us both a drink and waited for her to tell the truth about Aunty Dot. But she remained silent. It was as though she was listening to another conversation. I raised my voice to get her attention.

"DOREEN. You did know her didn't you."

She smiled, picked up her mug and took a sip.

"No dear. I never met her. But one thing I do know is that she loved you very much and to be honest she thinks you can do better than The Rushbridge Gazette."

Once again that was exactly the sort of thing Aunt Dot would say. She never pulled any punches, always spoke her mind.

"But how?...How do you know all this?"

That's when she said the famous line. Though I very much doubt if she'd ever seen the film.

"I see dead people. They talk to me, tell me things. I don't see them clearly, just as shadows. Dead people don't like to be seen as they are now, so they make your eyes go weak. But I hear them. Clear as day. Your Aunt Dot is here now standing right behind you. She just said you won't believe me."

Again she laughed as she said those last few words and she was right to laugh. I didn't believe her, not a word. There must be something else. I decided to put her to the test.

"Okay. Ask Aunt Dot to tell you something that only she and I would know."

Her eyes moved to look at something to my left. She squinted as if trying to focus. Then she nodded.

"Okay. I understand. "

Now she looked back at me.

"After your Mum passed, Dot took you on holiday to Cornwall. You had ice cream but tripped over and it landed in the sand. You were inconsolable and cried for hours. She always thought it had nothing to do with the ice cream but more about your Mum."

That was it. I was hooked. As impossible as it all seemed, I suddenly believed in Doreen Lucas.

For the next hour she told me about Ivan and his Russian lessons. He'd been visiting for many years. Usually twice a week and during that time he'd taught her the language. She also told me about the many "visitors" she had. Random dead people would just pop in to say hello and talk to her. She never left the house anymore because there were just too many distractions. Apparently dead people are everywhere.

After another mug each of whisky she stopped talking and looked away. She was listening.

"Yes, yes, why not. I'd be happy to help."

I wasn't sure if she was talking to me or someone else. I couldn't help but interrupt.

"What?

"You're Aunty Dot has a plan to help you get a better job."

Doreen went on to explain what Dot had in mind. If it worked I would be famous. So of course I agreed.

That was a few months ago. I've been visiting 58 Woodbridge Gardens twice a week since then. I sit with Doreen while she talks and listens to the guests that arrive. It's amazing how many dead people want to come and tell her things. We've had musicians, politicians, gangsters, religious leaders, even royalty.

I sit and make notes as she repeats what they tell her. She can even ask for certain people to attend. It takes a day or two but they do come. Ever eager to tell their stories.

I'm still with the Rushbridge Gazette. But not for long. Tomorrow I have an interview with a large Sunday Newspaper as an Investigative Journalist. How can they turn me down? I've got this amazing story about Lord Lucan. I can prove where he went after the murder of his nanny and even where his body is buried. All done with proper investigative techniques of course. After I've got the job I'll start to explain other unsolved mysteries like what happened to jimmy Hoffa and who really shot JFK. It's a wonderful opportunity.

There's just one drawback. I'm beginning to think I can hear the voices as well. But not clearly, just as faint whispers. Oh and another thing. My reading glasses don't seem to work anymore...

Jimmy Kid Taylor

"Look Tommy, I could have gone another two rounds. The ref stepped in too early. I..."

He was interrupted by his Manager, Tommy Seabrook. A tough east Londoner who didn't mince his words.

"Fuck off. Don't kid yourself Jim. He beat you. He was all over you in the ninth. The ref had to stop it. It's over. Time to call it a day."

The words hit him like a sledgehammer. Retirement had never been mentioned before. He came back the only way he knew. Fighting. He lunged at Tommy Seabrook and grabbed him tight by his collar and tie.

"What the fuck do you mean by that? I'm twenty nine for fucks sake. I'm in my prime. I'm three fights away from a title fight and you've got the balls to tell me to call it a day? Fuck off Tommy. Just fuck off!"

He let him go, moved away and sat down on an old wooden stool in the corner of the dressing room. Annoyed with himself for losing his temper.

Tommy straightened his tie. Took a deep breath. Realising that his words may have been a bit harsh. He waited for a few seconds before he spoke again. This time his voice was quiet and slow.

"Look Jim. Gonzalez beat you fair and square tonight. The ref stepped in because he was worried you were taking too many punches. No way will we get a rematch. He's moving on. Already lined up a bout with Romero. That's a title eliminator. He wins that and he gets his shot at Suarez for the title."

Jimmy's head dropped into his chest.

"Okay, okay, just line me up a couple of easy fights and I'll bide my time till I get another chance."

Tommy shook his head.

"Jim, listen to me. You know the rules of this game, whether it's inside or outside the ring you never, ever, take a step backwards, you've always got to keep going forward. You start fighting nobodies and you become a fucking nobody."

Jim heard Tommy's words but was lost in his own thoughts. He'd been British Lightweight Champion at just twenty three. European Champion at twenty six. Jimmy "Kid" Taylor was the golden boy of British Boxing. Unbeaten in all amateur and professional fights. No one went more than eight rounds with Jimmy the Kid. Then he fought the world number four, a Mexican called Garcia. This guy was different to anyone he'd ever fought. His punches were accurate, crisp, sharp and everyone of them felt as though he was being pummelled with a ball hammer. He won on points, but his body was never quite the same. He pissed blood for two weeks after. The spiteful punches to the kidneys had taken their toll. The vision in his right eye was permanently blurred, something he'd never told Tommy, and he was now partially deaf in his right ear. But he won and that was all that mattered. He took ten months off hoping to fight Suarez for the World title. But Suarez was busy fighting the world ranked number two. So Tommy decided the big money fight would be a re-match with Garcia. Big mistake. This time Garcia destroyed him in three rounds. He couldn't see Garcia's left hand punches until it was too late because of the poor vision in his right eye. He was on the canvas six times in three rounds. He was in hospital for five days after the fight. But was training again within three months. Then tonight he'd fought Gonzalez and the ref stopped it in the ninth. He'd taken another beating and lost.

He cleared his head and looked up at Tommy. They'd been together for thirteen years. He knew exactly what buttons to press to get what he wanted.

"Yeh, I know the rules Tom and I agree. Lightweight is no good for me. But think about this just for a second. What if I put on five pounds and move up to Welterweight. *THAT* Division is wide open. AND there's that new kid from Lewisham who's knocking everyone out. How about lining up a fight for me and him. Would be a great British fight. You'd sell out Wembley for that one. Maybe even get the TV guys interested?"

He could hear the wheels going round in Tommy Seabrooks head. He'd just suggested something that could make Tommy a lot of money. He knew what the answer would be. He watched as Tommy nodded his head.

"Well, as long as you're sure Jim. This Lewisham boy is good, hits hard, great left hand, quick, fast, accurate and agile. But he's never fought anyone of your class before. Okay let me see what I can do."

Tommy walked over to Jimmy and patted him on the back. He said something to Jim as he left. But Jimmy Kid Taylor never heard him. He was now completely deaf in his right ear.

Four weeks of rest, sunshine and recuperation were followed by three months of hard training. Jimmy Kid Taylor was ready.

Ready to face his next opponent. The young Bobby Jones from Lewisham.

The extra weight he was carrying felt good. He felt strong, confident and quick. His damaged right eye didn't seem to be a problem. Luckily Bobby Jones was a southpaw which meant he would jab with his right hand which would land on the left side of Jimmys face. So all the sparring had been done with Southpaw fighters and Jim had been careful to protect his right eye at all times.

Tommy Seabrook had done his job well. Wembley was a sell out and ITV were showing it live at 10.30pm. It was being billed as the British fight of the decade, a title eliminator. The winner would go on to fight for the Welterweight Championship of the World.

They both stood in the middle of the ring. The referee gave them his instructions, not that Jimmy heard a word of them, and they returned to their corners. The bell rang and they both rushed to the centre of the ring and that's when Jimmy Kid Taylor realised he had a big problem. Bobby Jones had changed his stance from Southpaw to Orthodox.

Thirty seconds later ITV stopped their coverage of the boxing and returned to the studio. The announcer, visibly shaken, composed himself and said.

"Distressing scenes at Wembley. We hope and pray for Jimmy Kid Taylor."

Rules Are Rules

Our family have rules. And they're simple rules. You hurt us and we'll hurt you back. But double time.

You disrespect me and mine and we'll have a problem. Call me or my family a name and I'll break your windows, do it again and I'll break your face.

Your kid hurts one of mine and I'll come round and put all of yours in the hospital.

You get the picture? Don't mess with me and mine.

But some people don't get it in one. They think the rules don't apply to them. They're wrong. Take Mark Reynolds for example.

Mark was a big man. Stood six feet seven inches and weighed around twenty stone. A face on the local estate. But his lad hit mine. Not just that but he kicked the shit out of him when he was on the floor and busted his leg and arm. Now, my lads no angel. He probably deserved to get hit. But them aint the rules.

The rules are simple. You hurt anyone of us and we're gonna hurt you back.

Mark came round the next day. Tears in his eyes.

"They didn't know it was your boy. Honest. They didn't know."

I did the usual thing. Shook his hand. But we both knew what would happen.

His kid moved away. Went to stay with an Aunt in Liverpool. After a year he went to stay with another relation in Edinburgh. But one day he was found in a bad way. Close to death near a railway line.

I went round to Marks the next day. Shook his hand. "Even" was all I said. Mark just nodded.

So imagine my state of mind when my wife was mugged coming home one night. She'd stopped to get some money out of the cash machine at Asda's. As she walked away two guys threw her to the floor and took her bag.

She was in hospital for three days. Cuts, bruises and a dislocated shoulder.

Word got round. The two guys realised what they'd done and gave themselves up to the police. I pretended to let it go. But everyone knew what the consequences would be.

They went to trial and got two years suspended sentence. They screamed in court. They WANTED to go to Prison. But they were let out and back on the streets. They even asked for Police protection.

Fair play to the old bill, they ignored them. They were scum. If truth be known I think the boys in blue wanted to see them get their comeuppance.

I waited. No rush. It was eighteen months before anything happened. One of the guys had fucked off to Spain. Didn't matter, we found him. Just by total coincidence he was also mugged, coming home late one night from a club. Nasty business, blood everywhere. Whoever did it took his money but also slit his throat.

Me? I was indoors watching Strictly Come Dancing.

Two months later and the other one jumps from one of the Tower Blocks on the Langley Estate. Nothing to do with me...really. He just jumped rather than wait for the inevitable.

So, a new family has moved into the street, just four doors up. The Donovans. I know them for two reasons. Firstly, by reputation and secondly...well, I'll tell you about that a bit later.

Joe Donovan has a haulage firm and his two boys work with him. I hear they're a bit of a handful, all of them, even Mrs Donovan. She bit a chunk out of her neighbours ear during a fight over a garden fence panel. When I first heard the story I didn't think much of it. Woman fight, so what? But then I discovered that her neighbour was Jack Williams, a six foot five scaffolder. Respect...

Now everyone around here knows about my rules. Leave us alone and you'll be fine. Mess with us and you'll be in a world of trouble. Simple, easy to follow. Over the years some people have broken those rules and they've paid the consequences. Their fault, not mine.

I'm sure the Donovans know all about us, just as we know of them. But, just to make sure there's no misunderstanding I've arranged a "Sit down" tonight with Joe at the Royal Oak pub.

Best to get things straight from the outset. We don't want another "Chandler" situation!

Oh you don't know about the Chandlers?

Well they were another "Big" family that moved onto the Estate a couple of years ago. Came with a reputation for being a bit handy. I didn't explain the rules to them, just assumed they knew.

Bob Chandler sold cars. My boy hadn't long passed his test and wanted a run around. Nothing flash, just reliable. Bob sold him a Ford Focus. A few months later and it needs an MOT. My boy takes it into a garage, the mechanic looks it over and tells him that it's a cut and shunt. That's two cars that have been welded together. An accident waiting to happen. A death trap.

My boy goes to Bob and asks for his money back. Bob tells him to fuck off. He didn't think the rules applied to him. He was wrong.

Apart from selling cars, Bob Chandler was a keen Pigeon fancier. Had a massive loft at the end of his garden. He raced them, bred them and showed them. Some were champions worth thousands of pounds.

I was in Majorca on holiday when his loft caught fire. People tell me the smell was like burnt barbeque chicken and hung in the air for days.

The Police asked him if he could think of anyone that had a grudge against him. Bob gave them my name and told them there'd been a dispute over a car. Fair play to the Old Bill, they suggested Bob gave me my money back. Unfortunately he declined.

The Chandlers moved away after Bob was involved in a freak accident. He was under one of his cars one day checking the exhaust. The jack slipped and poor Bob got a bit mangled.

They live in Kent now. I know the address because he still hasn't paid my boy his money back. I'll wait for him to start walking again before I take it any further.

So you understand my reasoning about the "Sit down" tonight with Joe Donovan.

Oh, and the second reason I know the Donovans? My daughter has just started going out with Joes youngest son. Best behave himself...cos Rules are rules.

The Toenail

Dave and Ronny were in their most favourite place in the whole world, the Captain Kidd pub in Wapping. Dave was leaning on the big old wooden bar and, as usual, was holding court.

Dave called over to Ted the landlord.

"Oi Ted, did you hear what was washed up on the other side of the river by The Nelson Pub?"

Ted came over looking intrigued.

"What was it Dave, body part?"

By now a few of the other regulars had gathered round, all curious to find out what had been washed up. Dave continued.

"Well I've got a mate that works for the River Police and he gave me all the info."

Ronny took a swig of his pint then asked the same question that Ted had.

"So go on Dave what was it, torso, head, what?"

Dave leaned forward and looked right and left as though he was about to tell some great secret.

"Toenail!"

Ted was the first to laugh.

"Fucking Toenail is that it, so what, not much they can deduce from a fucking toenail!"

Dave didn't laugh. He face was serious.

"You'd be surprised Ted, technology these days is amazing."

One of the other regulars ordered a round of drinks. Ronny took a swig of his beer and turned to look at Dave.

"This isn't going to be another one of your *STORIES* is it Dave, like last week when you told us that you used to train Dolphins in the Thames."

Dave was indignant.

"That was true, thirty years ago the Thames was full of Dolphins, they used to come in through the estuary at Southend, get lost and before they knew it they were up by bloody Tower Bridge, someone had to get in there with them and show them the way back, there was a team of us back then all qualified Dolphin Trainers, we'd turn then and get them back to the coast. If it wasn't for the barrier the Thames would be full of the fuckers!"

Ronny and Ted laughed but a couple of the other regulars were nodding as though they agreed with Dave. He continued.

"Anyway, they took the toenail off to forensics, from the size and shape of the nail they can tell what toe it's from, this toenail was from the toe next to the big one. They can also estimate the size of the toe and from this can tell what size foot it came from. This was a size nine."

Ronny and Ted were now a bit unsure, this sounded possible. Ted had another sip of his beer eager for some more info.

"And?"

Dave knew he had them and carried on.

"Well because it's a size nine, they know that it's a man's foot and not a woman, it's extremely rare for a woman to have such large feet."

One of the other regulars piped up.

"That's right, I've been married five times and have got six daughters none of them have bigger than a seven."

Everyone agreed. Dave went on.

"Now the size of the foot is very important, you can estimate the weight and height of a person from it, for example you wouldn't get a twenty stone man with a size six foot would you, never be able to carry the weight would it?"

Everyone agreed. Made perfect sense.

"So they estimated that the man was five foot nine and weighted around eleven and a half stone"

Ronny was impressed.

"Fuck me that's amazing, all that from a fucking toe nail!"

Dave nodded eager to continue.

"That's not all. They can tell the man's age as well. You see the toenail is made up of calcium, the calcium in the nail forms little ridges along the nail, if you count the ridges it gives you the age of the person!"

Ted was the first to react.

"Like a tree, when you count the rings in its trunk to find out how old it is."

Everyone agreed. Dave was quickly back in full flow.

"Exactly the same principle Ted, well spotted, this man was thirty eight when he died."

Ted started to pour another round of drinks for everyone. Ronny passed them round and was eager for Dave to continue.

"How do they know he died Dave, couldn't it just be that someone lost a nail while working on the Thames?"

Dave was grateful for the new pint and gulped down half of it in one go.

"Decay, Ted, decay. You see the nail had dirt attached to it, the scientists determined that the dirt was from the 1880's, it's all to do with the clay and sand element, it's all very technical but they think that this nail had definitely been in the Thames since the 1880's."

There was a silence for a few seconds before Ronny decided to give everyone a summary.

"So what you're saying Dave is that from a single toenail, they have discovered that a man in 1880, who was thirty eight, weighed eleven and a half stone and was five foot nine died somehow in the Thames?"

Dave was chuffed with himself.

"Yep Ron, all that from one tiny toenail, amazing isn't it?"

Everyone agreed, and pondered this information whilst they took large gulps of their beer. But Dave wasn't finished, he had more information to give.

"You think that's clever, they now know that his name was Edward and he came from Bermondsey!"

Ted almost spat out his pint!

"How the fuck........?"

Dave was quick to interrupt.

"This is the brilliant bit, they searched through all the London Newspapers from the early 1880's, they found an article in the Dockers paper "The Wharf". It was dated 18th February 1882, it said that a Lighterman had fallen into the Thames and his body hadn't been found, his name was Edward Barnes and he lived in Bermondsey, he was thirty eight years old, he was five foot nine and weighed eleven stone six pounds and he took size nine shoes, apparently Channel Five are doing a documentary on it"

Ronny ordered another round.

"Dave, that is an incredible story, I thought at first you were making it up, but it all makes perfect sense, can't wait to see it on the TV, unbelievable what they can do these days!"

Dave was pleased with himself and decided to go one step further.

"Yep, they've also traced his descendants and are going to present his remains to them at a special memorial service at St Georges Cathedral in Southwark later this year, The Mayor is gonna be there and everything."

Ted raised his glass.

"Here's to old Edward Barnes, god rest his soul."

The whole pub raised their glasses, cheered and drank to the late great Edward Barnes!

Dave was still smiling when he left the pub an hour later. He'd sunk six pints and two large whiskeys and hadn't bought a single round.

Boy did he love that pub...and of course the regulars!

Job On The Tills

"Could Jim Dawson please report to Mister Draper's office. Jim Dawson to Mister Draper's office please."

Jim heard his name being called over the tannoy. Sixteen years at Thorogoods DIY and this was the first time his name had been called. He suddenly felt important. Mister Draper was a busy man, a senior management man. He was only one position below the owner, Mister Thorogood. Maybe it was promotion.

He'd spent his first eleven years in the warehouse checking stuff in and out, moving stock around and of course sweeping up. He was very proud of his clean warehouse and knew every inch of it inside out. Then, for the past five years he'd moved up to shop floor. He now made sure that the shelves were stacked properly, everything in its place and priced correctly. He even had to point people in the right direction around the store. It was a big store and people got confused, lost even. They would often ask him where a certain colour of paint would be or where they kept the hand tools. All the regulars knew him and some of them even asked for him by name. They would come in and say "Hi Jim, where can I find a screw that will fit this hinge." He always knew the answer. He knew where everything was in the store. It was important work.

He began to think that maybe because of all his hard work and loyalty he would now be promoted to the returns section or even trained on the tills!

With a wide grin on his face and hope in his heart he made his way up the stairs and along the narrow corridor to Mister Draper's office. He knocked on the door.

"Come in!"

A loud voice boomed from inside the office. Jim entered. A large red faced man around forty years of age with grey slicked back hair and big round spectacles was sitting at a desk in front of him.

"Ahh Jim, thanks for coming so promptly. Please take a seat."

Jim smiled and sat down opposite Mister Draper.

"I suppose you're wondering why I've called you up here, eh Jim?"

"Yes Sir."

"Well, times are a changing Jim. We're not as popular as we used to be. What with B&Q and Wickes and all the other bastard stores that want to sell what we sell for a fraction of the bloody cost. So we need to make changes. With me so far Jim?"

Jims face hadn't changed. He still had a smile across his face. Waiting for the words *"TILLS"* or *"RETURNS"* to come out of Mister Draper's mouth.

"Yes Sir."

"Good man Jim, good man. That makes it a lot easier. I knew you'd understand. So we need to make some adjustments to our staffing levels. So we're letting you go Jim. You'll get a redundancy payment, statutory of course, nothing more, we're not a charity after all. Any questions Jim?"

Jim was still smiling. He hadn't heard a thing after "letting you go."

"Go where?"

"Sorry Jim, don't follow?"

"You said you were letting me go, go where?"

"Well that's up to you of course Jim. I'm sure you'll find something. You're only, what, fifty two?"

"Fifty three."

"Whatever. You'll be fine."

The enormity of what was happening began to slowly sink in. Jim's face changed.

"So I'm not getting a job on the tills then?"

Mister Draper looked confused and slightly angry. He shook his head.

"Of course you're not getting a bloody job on the tills. Those jobs are for people who can count Jim and have some kind of intelligence. You're being made *REDUNDANT*."

"But I've been with you for sixteen years."

"Now, now Jim, let's not argue about that. You've only had continued service for the last four years."

"But I started with the company sixteen years ago."

"Jim, look, five years ago you wanted to take your old mum to Australia, right?"

"Yes, to visit my elder brother who had cancer."

"You took two months off work. Is that correct?"

"Yes. But you said I could come back after my break."

"Which was very good of us Jim. I remember you being very grateful at the time. But it does mean that you had a BREAK in your service with us. Basically, you left and then you were re-employed two months later. This means that there was a BREAK in your service. So your redundancy will only be for the last four years."

"Oh, I didn't realise that I'd left when I went to Australia. I thought you were just letting me have some time off to visit family. I did think it was odd though when I had to fill in all that paperwork when I came back. Besides it's five, not four years.

"No Jim. Redundancy is only for FULL years. So since you returned to us, you've been working for four years and eleven months, so we don't count the eleven months. I know it's tough Jim but there's a recession on and we all have to do our bit. No point in worrying about a petty eleven months is there now. The LAW says we have to do everything by the book. Now you'll get a week and a halves pay for every full year since your BREAK in service. So that's six weeks wages."

Mister Draper started tapping on a calculator.

"Now then, you are on two hundred and one pounds ninety two pence a week. So you'll get one thousand two hundred and eleven pounds and fifty two pence. Not bad eh Jim?"

"Is that it?"

"I think you're being rather ungrateful here Jim. You could take your Mum to see your brother again in Australia with the money?"

"He died three years ago and Mum's now house bound due to her illness."

"Whatever. You could take yourself away on a nice break somewhere."

"But who would look after Mum?"

"That's down to you Jim, all I'm saying is that you'll be getting a nice cheque and you should be very grateful and do something with it. Now then that's it and I wish you all the best for the future."

Mister Draper stood up and put out his hand. Jim stood up and automatically shook it. He still wasn't sure what was happening.

"So what happens now? When do you let me go?"

"Now Jim, now. No point in hanging around. It's Friday anyway and you've only got two hours before your shift finishes so we'll let you off those couple of hours. Seems only fair. Go home Jim and everything will come through the post in a couple of days. Goodbye and good luck, please close the door on your way out."

Mister Draper sat back down again and started looking at some paperwork. Jim stood there for a moment, then turned round to leave the office.

Then he did something. Something that took him by surprise. He didn't know why he did it but he seemed not to be in control of his actions. It was as if someone was working him by remote control and he had no option but to follow the instructions. He closed Mister Draper's door and noticed that the key was in the lock on the outside. He very slowly and quietly turned the key, locking Mister Draper inside.

He walked along the corridor, down the stairs and into the warehouse. He made his way to the paint storage area. He picked up a two litre plastic bottle of white spirit and emptied its contents onto the hundreds of cans of oil based paints. He knew this section well. It was the only blind spot in the whole of the warehouse completely out of view of the CCTV cameras. He lit a match and flicked it onto the tins then calmly walked away.

He heard the explosion a few seconds later. It must have been the loud noise that jolted him back to reality. He ran to the front of the building and begun helping his colleagues escape through the thick black smoke.

The fire at Thorogoods was the largest the county had seen in over fifty years. Sixteen fire engines were needed to bring it under control. The whole building burnt to the ground. All staff were accounted for except one. A Mister Reginald Draper the General Manager. He could only be identified by dental records.

Jim Dawson became a local hero. Mister Thorogood himself paid tribute to his bravery. "If it wasn't for the quick actions of this loyal employee the loss of life could have been far greater."

When Thorogoods re-opened three months later, Jim was promoted. He now had his job on the tills.

Old Mister Thorogood didn't know why, but he had a strange feeling that it was best to give Jim Dawson exactly what he wanted.

Eleven Plus

Seeing the GCSE results on the TV the other day reminded me of an exam I took in 1969. It was called the Eleven- plus. It was an exam that all Eleven year olds sat in their last year in Junior School. It was to assess whether you were talented enough to go to a Grammar School.

I was a bright kid at eight and nine and when I was ten I remember my teacher telling my proud parents at an "open" evening that he fully expected me to pass the Eleven plus. I'd come "Top of the class" two years running and now I was approaching my final year at Junior School.

I didn't know what to expect in the eleven plus exam and to be honest neither did my parents. Their schooling had been severely interrupted by the inconvenience of war and evacuation.

The teachers didn't seem to know much about the eleven plus either, mainly because no child had ever passed it at my school. My school was in the middle of a rough working class council estate. And to add to that, it was also the worst school in the Borough.

Mum decided to encourage my academic career and bought a full set of Encyclopaedias at a local jumble sale. It took her five trips from the local church hall to get them home. There were 12 volumes and they weighed a ton. They were a few years out of date (1948) but that didn't matter, they were full of useful knowledge. Mum said I should flick through them and read things that I was interested in. I didn't need much encouragement, I loved reading and quickly found stuff of interest.

Yes, the way forward it seemed was to read stuff from the Encyclopaedias.

I had six months until the exam. Every night I would choose a volume and flick through it and read large chunks about "things".

A few "things" really interested me and I was sure they would come up in such an important exam as the Eleven plus.

The first thing was an Albatross. I quickly learnt that there were 22 species of Albatross, the biggest being the Wandering Albatross with a wing span of an incredible twelve feet. That's the size of two bedroom doors apparently...amazing stuff. Then there's the Sooty Albatross, not as big as the Wandering but still a big bird. Yep, I could name all twenty two and give you their wingspan. How clever was I?

Another "thing" that caught my eye was a man called Napoleon. I'd never heard of him before but soon learnt all about the French Revolution, his Famous battles, when and where he was born and where he eventually died. Someone as important as Napoleon would surely be in the Eleven-plus.

Then there was British Cattle. Wow, there were a lot of those. I read mainly about The Aberdeen Angus. It can weigh over a ton and is either Black or Red in colour. And...it's from Scotland!

Armed with all this extraordinary information I went in to sit the exam supremely confident.

Mr Wilson gave out the papers. I couldn't wait to have a look at the questions and get started. I was sure no one else in that room would have the knowledge that I had.

He blew a whistle. This meant that we could turn over our papers and begin.

I remember the first question vividly. It asked what were the four points of the compass. I knew the answer of course. North, South, East and West but what one was at the top or bottom or left or right I hadn't a clue. I flicked through to find the questions about Albatross's, or Napoleon or British Cattle. To my absolute astonishment there wasn't any! Not one...

I failed my Eleven-Plus, along with everyone else in my class.

Can't think why...

Uncle Frank Swam The Channel

Uncle Frank swam the channel. That's what I was told when I was a kid. Not by him, but by his wife, my Aunty Flo. She'd be in the kitchen cooking Sunday dinner and we'd all be sitting at the big table in the room next door. She'd say the same thing every week. "You lot better eat all this up or you won't get big and strong like your Uncle Frank. He swam the channel you know!"

Uncle Frank would just raise his eyebrows and look slightly embarrassed. He never commented on it.

My earliest recollection of Uncle Frank was when I was five years old. He was the biggest man I'd ever seen and just looking at him made me cry. I'd run to mum for a cuddle whenever he entered the room frightened to look at the giant that wanted to pick me up.

But by the time I was seven he was my favourite of all the great Uncles and I'd look forward to our visits to their large house in Stamford Hill, North London. He was married to my Granddads younger sister, Florence. Although her name was posh, "Flo" certainly wasn't. She could swear better than most men and could down a pint of beer in seconds. I never saw her without a cigarette hanging out the corner of her mouth. Flo was a formidable woman. Frank on the other hand was a gentle giant. Well over six feet tall with hands the size of shovels. Car mechanic by trade, he could strip an engine down, clean every piston and valve and put it back together again in just a few hours on a Saturday afternoon.

They never had kids of their own. Flo had been a bit of a wild child in her teens and secretly visited a lady who did something quite extraordinary with knitting needles. Her "insides" were never the same. By the time she met Frank she knew she couldn't have children. I suppose that's why they treated Mum and Dad so well, they were like the kids they never had and me and my sister were like their own Grandchildren.

After dinner on Sundays we'd play cards at the big table. We'd play Whist, Solo, Pairs and Newmarket. Then Uncle Frank would go and get the Shove ha'penny board and challenge me to a game. He always won! As we left, Aunt Flo would give us each a bright shiny silver half crown. "Ice cream money." She'd say.

I was twelve years of age when he died in 1970. I remember the day well. I came home from school and Mum was crying in the kitchen. I asked her what was wrong. "Your Uncle Frank's had a heart attack. He's passed away." He was just fifty four.

For some reason I can't explain, I wanted to go to the funeral. I'd never been to one before. I'd had old Aunts and Uncles die before and my Granddad was buried just the previous year, I'd never thought about going to any of those. Besides, funerals weren't a place for kids in our family. But Uncle Frank was different, I felt as though I "needed" to go. To my surprise, Dad agreed.

I remember sitting on a long wooden bench alongside Mum and Dad in a Church somewhere in North London. Uncle Franks Coffin was in front of us and we sang hymns. A man I'd never seen before stood up and walked to the front, he put his hand on the coffin and started to speak.

"Me and Frank were mates. Good mates. We signed up on the same day. Did our training together and soon found ourselves in France fighting the Germans."

He paused, composed himself and carried on.

"Things didn't go according to plan over there and we ended up on sitting on a beach waiting to be picked off by German planes. There were thousands of us. None of us really sure what was going on or what we should do. After three days a rumour started to spread that boats would soon be arriving to take us back to England. All we had to do was wait."

He looked at the coffin and smiled.

"But Frank wasn't convinced. At twenty four he was the oldest of our small group and by far the biggest. We all looked up to Frank, literally! He kept saying the longer we waited the more chance we had of being gunned down on the beaches. Frank had a plan. He'd swim back to England. It was only twenty or so mile, he was sure he'd make it. We all thought he was mad or just larking about, but first thing the next morning Frank put down his rifle, took off his belt and heavy boots and started walking towards the sea. We saw him wade in and start swimming. It wasn't long before he was out of sight. To be honest I never expected to see him again. It was another day before the rest of us were lined up and marched into the sea. We could see small ships in the distance and only my head was above water by the time I got to one of them. It was a small fishing boat out of Gravesend. Two blokes hauled me aboard and gave me a blanket. They took as many of us as they could then turned around and headed for Dover."

Again he stopped and looked at the coffin before continuing.

"And guess who was there waiting for me? Thousands of men all along the seafront, utter chaos everywhere and who was the first person I see? Yep...me old mate Frank. Large as life, with a big smile on his face."

He paused for a few seconds.

"Did he really swim the channel? I have no idea because he never spoke about it. Every time I mentioned it he just shrugged his shoulders and changed the subject. But you know what? I'd like to think he did."

He gently tapped the coffin then sat back down.

That was almost fifty years ago and I think about Uncle Frank often. He swam the channel you know.

The Invitation

Bob Jenkins retired early at just fifty five. He and his wife Linda were financially secure. His thirty five years with the Post Office had earned him a nice pension and a generous lump sum. Now, he spent his days doing voluntary work for his local British Legion Club. He cleaned the toilets every morning, served behind the bar at lunchtimes and every year sold more Poppies than anyone else in the county.

His reward for this tireless service, and his many years in the Territorial Army, was an invitation for him and Linda to attend a posh dinner at The Guildhall in London. These invitations were like gold dust and only sent out to people who were connected to the Armed Forces in some way. To receive one was a great honour. They were surrounded in secrecy. Mainly because they were hosted by a member of the Royal family. This year Princess Anne would be in attendance.

Bob kept the invitation safe in the top drawer of his bedside cabinet. Every few days he would take it out and look proudly at his name written in gold leaf. Today he noticed something. It seemed to be coming apart. He carefully picked at one corner and realised that his invitation had another one stuck to the back of it. After a few minutes of gentle manipulation, they came unstuck. The extra invitation was in the name of Mr and Mrs Richard Denning.

That's when Bob rang me.

"Hi Jim. What you and Doreen doing tomorrow night?"

I smiled. I thought he was going to invite us to another one of his boozy barbeques.

"Nothing mate, why what you thinking of?"

Bob went on to explain in some detail about the extra invitation. I wasn't keen. It seemed risky.

"But what about Richard Denning? Won't he be wondering where his invitation is?"

Bob laughed.

"No you crumpet. These invitations are sent out in secret. You don't know you've been invited until the invitation turns up. Richard Denning won't have a clue about the dinner. He'll be none the wiser. Besides, it's tomorrow night. It's too late for me to send the invitation back and too late for it to find its way to Richard Denning. If you don't come they'll just be two spare seats. It's black tie, four course meal with wine, a live band with a free bar. Princess Anne is going to be there!"

I thought about it for a few seconds, and with a bit more persuasion from Bob, decided to take the chance.

"Okay. We'll come. "

The following evening the four of us shared a cab and went off to Guildhall. I was still nervous about the whole thing and desperate for Bob to reassure me that everything would be okay.

"Look Bob, you sure we're doing the right thing?"

Bob did his usual...he laughed.

"It'll be fine. There's a champagne reception when we arrive. Then we sit down to eat. We're all on the same table so we'll keep close. If anyone asks you about yourself just be vague. Say you help out at the local British Legion and do a lot of charity work, just don't get too bogged down in detail. After the meal they'll be some speeches. Princess Anne will probably thank everyone for their loyal service to the armed forces. Then the band strikes up, we get up and dance and have free drinks all night. Easy!"

I still had my doubts.

"But what if someone knows Richard Denning?"

Bob put his hand on my shoulder.

"Look mate there are hundreds of thousands of people connected with the Armed Forces. Soldiers past and present. People are chosen from all sections of the service. Take me for example. There are more than 2500 British Legion branches in the UK. I don't know anyone else that's been invited so I'll know no one. It'll be the same for Richard Denning. He'll just be someone that was chosen at random. Trust me. It'll be fine."

We arrived and walked into a grand banqueting hall. A man in uniform welcomed us and took our invitations. He looked at them closely and then handed them to another man who nodded and walked away. The man in uniform shook our hands.

"A very warm welcome Mr Denning and Mr Jenkins. You are both on table twelve. Please help yourself to a glass of Champagne and enjoy the rest of your evening. "

Bob winked at me as we walked away.

"See... told you it would be okay."

We all took a glass of champagne and for the first time I began to relax.

The place began to fill up. Women were dressed in ball gowns and the men were either dressed in Dinner Suits with bow tie of their full military uniform. I'd never seen so many medals in all my life.

Princess Anne took her seat at the top table along with other impressive looking dignitaries.

The four course meal was exquisite. Thankfully the other people on our table seemed a bit stuffy and didn't really mingle. I was about to take a mouth full of coffee when I heard a bell ring and the lights dimmed. The man in uniform who welcomed us when we arrived was standing up. The room fell quiet.

"Good evening Ladies and Gentleman. I trust you all enjoyed your meal."

There was a nodding of heads and various noises of approval from the room. The man continued with his speech. He thanked everyone for their service to the armed forces and how we'd all deserved this special evening. He went on for about ten minutes. When he finished we all gave a round of applause.

You could hear a pin drop as Princess Anne got up from her chair and began to speak.

"Ten years ago this week a special mission was taking place in South Afghanistan. A small group of specially trained men were assigned to destroy a bomb making factory in Helmand. The operation was compromised and these brave men found themselves in an extremely difficult situation. Sadly only one of this elite group survived, but he was captured and spent three days in the hands of the enemy. In the dead of night he managed to escape and somehow, miraculously after seven days in the desert he found his way back to camp. Because of the secrecy and delicate nature of this operation this brave soldier was never given the full recognition that he deserved. Well tonight we intend to change that situation. I am delighted to award the highest medal of gallantry, The Victoria Cross to...Captain Richard Denning!"

I felt the spotlight on me. I was aware of people standing up around me and the sound of applause. All I could think of was..."Oh FUCK."

Top Of The Tree

In 1994 I changed profession. I decided to become a Financial Advisor. Two of my mates were doing it and earning some serious money. I had to sit a few exams of course, Financial Planning Certificates they were called, but they were a breeze. I passed and was let loose on the general public. I worked for a large Estate Agent and became their Mortgage Advisor. Anyone wanting to buy a house through them had to see me first. Those were the rules and it worked like a dream.

If they already had a mortgage, no problem. I would beat the deal they were on and show them a cost saving that they just couldn't ignore. If they didn't have a mortgage in place, no problem, I would sort one out for them with one of my contacts at the local Building Society or Bank. Any Endowments, Insurance or Pension products they needed I would arrange and take the commission. In a good week I was arranging three a day and earning some serious money.

I soon got a reputation for being a bit of a "fixer". I was the man people came to if they'd been turned down by other Financial Advisors.

You see I soon realised that EVERYONE has targets, and if they don't achieve those targets they don't get their bonus. And in some cases, they might even lose their jobs.

Take the Manager of the local Building Society. He has a lending target set by his boss. Let's imagine the target is one million pounds. This means that he *WANTS* to lend people money. In fact, he *HAS* to lend them money or he doesn't get his bonus. So what does he do? He encourages people like me to place their Mortgages with him and not another Building Society. He'll take me out for a few beers or get me tickets for Football matches, he'll even offer to let a few mortgages go through that perhaps shouldn't. He'll make sure that they get stamped "approved", but then get lost in a pile somewhere with a load of other applications.

People are desperate to buy they're houses, but sometimes it's obvious they can't really afford it. Doesn't matter. Lend them the money anyway. They always keep up to date for the first few months, it's only later that they realise that maybe they've bitten off more than they can chew. But by that time, everyone's hit their targets and bonuses have been paid.

That's just the way it was back then. Easy!

I remember one couple. They were in their late twenties. They'd seen a house they wanted and sat down with me to work out how they could afford it. He worked as a delivery driver on a low wage and she had a part time job at the local supermarket. They had no savings. No way could they afford to buy it. But I was a "fixer" I could do miracles. I made a few calls, asked a few favours and within forty-eight hours I'd arranged a 100% mortgage plus a personal loan to pay for all their expenses.

I can still see their faces when I gave them the good news. Pure joy! The man couldn't thank me enough. He kept saying "Top of the tree you are mate. Top of the tree."

My career lasted four years. In the end my conscience got the better of me and I resigned.

But that was a long time ago. Things changed after the crash a few years back. We all knew it would happen. It was never an "If", it was always a "When."

I retired last year and now my days are filled with golf and having a few beers with mates. Today I'm in the pub with my best mate Danny. We played eighteen holes this morning and the first cold beer has gone down well. I'm about to order another round when I see a familiar face beside me.

"Any chance?" Words tumble from his mouth in desperation.

His skin is a strange shade of grey, his cheeks seem to be all bone and no flesh. His eyes are red and sunken. He looks as though he's just walked off the set of a Zombie film.

"I reach into my back pocket and pull out a twenty pound note and slide it along the counter.

"Here you go. Take a score. Pay me when you can.

He leans forward and for a brief moment I think he's going to hug me. But he pulls back at the last minute. I can see his eyes beginning to water.

"Thanks mate. Really appreciate it. I'll pay you back as soon as I can. I promise."

He turns away and takes a seat at the other end of the bar. Danny looks over at me and shakes his head.

"You are one soft touch you are."

I shrug.

"It's only money. He needs it and at the moment I can afford it. So why not?"

Danny gets up off of his bar stool and stands beside me.

"Because he's a fucking loser. That's why. You've just paid for his next fix. When that's gone he'll find another mug in another pub and pull the same scam. He's a fuck up!"

I ignore him and order two pints from the barmaid. She quickly delivers. I give her a big smile and look over at the man at the end of the bar.

"Get him a pint of whatever he wants."

Danny's jaw drops.

"Are you for real?"

The man gets his drink, looks over and raises his glass.

"Top of the tree you are mate. Top of the tree."

Room 7

"You're on the ground floor madam. Room 7. Straight along the corridor and it's the third room on the right. Welcome to The Wentworth."

The young receptionist smiled as she handed Tina Hawkins the key to her room.

"Will you be dining with us tonight?"

Tina never replied, just shook her head from side to side and headed towards the corridor. Room 7 was exactly where it was supposed to be, third door on the right. She turned the key in the lock and entered.

It was an average room in every way. Average price, average sized bed, average decor. That's all she needed. Nothing fancy was required. Besides, most of her time would be spent staring at the ceiling.

Her phone rang. She answered and heard an American accent.

"You there yet honey?"

"Yes. Just arrived. I'm in Room 7. Go past reception and it's the third door on the right."

"Good. I'm just pulling into the car park. See you in five minutes."

She knew nothing about this new punter, just that he was a rich American who was in town for a few days and wanted a bit of "fun." That's all the agency had told her. But they'd promised her eight hundred quid for just one evening. They'd even booked the Hotel room for her. She was guessing he'd probably paid them double what she was getting. That didn't matter, she could do with the money. Bobby needed new school shoes and the rent on the flat was due Friday.

She looked at herself in the bathroom mirror.

Not bad for thirty eight. She still had the looks of a woman in her late twenties. The gods had been kind and given her clear skin, high cheek bones, good teeth and a great set of lungs.

She threw back her blonde hair and let it settle naturally. Good to go.

She heard a knock. She stepped out of the bathroom and opened the door. In front of her was a short, overweight, middle aged man with grey hair and a big grin. He had a bottle of red wine in one hand and was carrying a small holdall in the other.

"Hey honey. What's your name?"

He walked past her, put the bottle on the table and the bag on the floor. He sat down on the bed. She closed the door and quickly made up a name.

"Stella."

His grin was now a full blown smile, showing a set of brownish crooked teeth.

"Nice to meet you. My name is Alan. Looks like I've gone and hit the jackpot with you Stella. You are one mighty fine looking woman."

He patted the bed with his left hand.

"Come and sit your pretty ass down here."

She had a choice to make. Sit down beside him, get started straightaway and get it over and done with. Or play for time and find out what he was into. She didn't want any surprises so took the second option.

"What's the rush? Let's open that wine first and have a drink."

He agreed.

"Sounds like a plan to me honey."

She picked up the bottle and unscrewed the top. She took two glasses from the bathroom, filled them up to the brim and handed one to him. He noticed her looking at his bag.

"I brought someone with me. Hope that's okay? The agency said it was!"

Her heart sank. What the fuck did he mean? She needed the money but there were limits as to what she was prepared to do for it. She took a large gulp of her wine and put on a brave smile.

"Someone?"

He picked up the bag and placed it on the bed. He slowly undid the zip and put his hand inside. Quick as a flash he brought out what looked like a huge rag doll. It had ginger hair, huge bulging eyes and a mouth as wide as its head. It seemed to be hanging from his arm. And then it spoke.

"Allo, my name is Gerald and this is my good friend Alan."

As the doll was saying the words she noticed Alan's lips moving. She'd had to deal with crazies before but this was just weird. The doll was staring at her...waiting. She spoke.

"Hello Gerald. My name is Stella. Pleased to meet you."

She wasn't sure if she should be looking at Alan or Gerald. But there was something about the dolls eyes that held her gaze. The other thing she noticed was the dolls lack of an American accent, if anything it sounded like a Londoner.

"Alan's a bit shy. But not me. I'm up for anything. Now why don't you two get started and I'll sit in the corner. I like to watch!"

Just when she thought the situation couldn't get any weirder... it did. Alan sat the dummy on a chair facing the bed and began to undress. He never said a word as he slipped out of his clothes and within seconds his podgy naked body was on full display. The doll shrieked.

"Come on love, get your kit off, let's see what you've got."

As the dummy was speaking she couldn't help look at Alan's face. He was good, his lips moved only slightly and he was able to throw his voice a fair way.

Again she made a quick decision in her head. All she had to do was have sex with the short podgy guy while an ugly looking doll sat in a chair in the corner, and looking at the state of Alan she was guessing it would all be over in just a few minutes. Yes it was all a bit weird, but she needed the eight hundred pounds badly. Decision made, she stripped naked and sat on the bed.

She heard the voice of Gerald again.

"Nice tits. Go on Alan old son. Fill your boots!"

She laid back and looked at the ceiling. Alan positioned himself on top and began his thrusting. As she expected it was all over in seconds. Alan rolled over and lay beside her. She looked over at the chair. The doll was gone.

She was aware of a noise at the bottom of the bed. She looked down and saw Gerald crawling towards her. Eyes and mouth wide open.

"MY TURN NOW!"

The young girl on reception looked at her colleague.

"Did you hear a scream?"

The other girl just shrugged her shoulders.

"God knows what they get up to in those rooms..."

English Rose

The room was empty, apart from two chairs and a small table between them.

Two men entered the room. Each took a chair and sat down. The bigger of the two men was holding a pad and paper. He looked across the desk and spoke.

"So Jim, tell me the whole story. From the beginning."

Jim was relaxed. He sat back in his chair and put his feet up on the desk. He began.

"I'm not quite sure when it all started. Sometime in the summer of 2013 I suppose. Wow, five years ago now. Where did all that time go? Anyway, I was early for an appointment with a prospective client, so I decided to have a coffee in a nearby café. The appointment was at 12.30 and I had half an hour to waste. It was an up market café, one of those places where you can't just say you want a coffee. It has to be an Americano or Latte or Cappuccino or whatever bollocks they're talking. Anyway, I was sitting down at a table nursing my three pound cup of java, when I heard a soft female voice behind me."

"Excuse me sir, do you mind if I join you?"

Jim stopped and started to look into space as though he was remembering the moment. The larger man was eager for him to continue.

"That's good Jim. Very good. Now, what happened next?"

Jim snapped out of his trance and continued.

"I turned round expecting the voice to be aimed at someone else. But a young blonde haired girl was looking straight at me. She smiled. I stood up and moved the chair opposite out from under the table and she sat down."

"Thank you very much. I hate drinking coffee on my own. Do you work around here?"

"She had sparkling blue eyes that were as big as her smile. Her complexion was pale, quite white in fact, which made a change from seeing all the London girls with their fake tans. I said I didn't, I suppose I should have said more but I was still shocked at someone in central London wanting to talk to a complete stranger. It's just not something that we do. Then she said and did something that surprised me."

"I'm going for a job interview in an hour not far from here. Do you think I'm suitably dressed for an interview?"

"She stood up. She was wearing a white blouse with a short beige jacket over the top. Her skirt was mid length, just below the knee and she was wearing red flat shoes which matched her shade of lipstick. She looked gorgeous. In fact, stunning. I sat back in my chair while she did a twirl in front of me. Here was a girl in her mid- twenties who I had known for just a few seconds doing a fashion show for me in the middle of an empty London café. Bizarre. I told her she'd knock them dead in that outfit. She giggled and sat back down."

Again Jim stopped and remembered. He smiled then continued.

"We sat there drinking our coffees and she asked me what work I did. I told her that I was a salesman for a Stationary Company and that it was all very boring. She giggled and agreed."

"Yep that sounds really boring!"

"We both laughed. We'd known each other for just a few minutes but here we were laughing together as though we'd known each other for years. I asked her if she wanted another coffee but she declined."

"No thanks. Not unless they can put a brandy in it. I'm a bit nervous about the interview. "

"I looked at my watch. It was 12.10. I had an idea. I knew there was a pub just round the corner and cautiously asked if she wanted something a bit stronger to calm he nerves. She stood up and grabbed my hand. Her face lit up like a firework."

"Come on then. What you waiting for?"

"The Pub was called the Rose and Crown and I thought that was appropriate because she looked just like an English Rose."

The bigger man stopped writing on his note pad. There was a silence. Jim was deep in thought.

"Jim, Jim, what happened in the pub?"

Jim seemed to snap out of his thoughts and began again.

"I asked her what she wanted to drink. Did she really want a Brandy or maybe something else? She just laughed at me."

"I've never even tasted brandy. It was just something I saw in a movie once. A woman ordered a Brandy and coffee. It seemed to go together so well. No, I'll have a white wine please."

"So I ordered a bottle of Sancerre and two glasses and we took a table in the corner. We chinked glasses and she drank her wine down in just one go. I was amazed, I'd never seen a woman do that before. She just threw back her head and roared with laughter."

"I needed that. So mister stationary man, what's your name?"

"I told her my name was Jim and asked what her name was."

"Katherine. Katherine Weller. My friends call me Kathy. So you can call me Kathy as well."

"I poured out more wine and wished her luck in her interview. But we stayed in the pub till three O'clock. I missed my appointment and she missed her interview. I called my boss and said I was sick and was going home. We spent the rest of the afternoon walking around the streets of London. We had dinner in an Italian restaurant in Covent Garden. I'd never been so happy. She made me feel alive. I can't describe it. Up until that day I thought I had it all. Beautiful wife, two lovely kids, job, car, everything. But all that changed the day I met Kathy."

Jim went quiet. He stroked an imaginary beard on his face. Deep in thought. The larger man tapped his shoulder with his notepad.

"Come on Jim, so far so good. Tell me how the day ended."

Jim composed himself and continued his story.

"It was getting late. I suppose it was about ten o'clock. I had twenty missed calls on my phone. All from the wife. We were near Holborn Station. Kathy stopped walking and just stood there. I asked if she was okay. She looked at me. No, she STARED at me. Then put her hands on either side of my face and kissed me."

"Will you spend the night with me Jim? Please?"

"I was taken aback by that. Her giggle had gone and now there was vulnerability about her that I'd not seen before. How could I resist her? So I agreed. We walked to a nearby hotel and I booked us in under the name of Mister and Mrs E. Rose."

Once again Jim stopped talking and was lost in his thoughts. This time the bigger man shouted.

"Jim. JIM! Come on now, we're close. The big question is. If you were so in love with Kathy. Why did you kill her?"

Jim looked at him. An honest look on his face.

"That's easy. Because she asked me to."

The big man looked confused.

"Sorry Jim. I'm not sure I follow. She asked you to kill her?"

Jim nodded.

"Yes. We booked into the hotel under the names of Mr and Mrs E. Rose. She never did ask me why I used that name. We took the lift up to the third floor. The room was perfect. She kissed me as soon as the door was closed. Then we sat on the bed and talked. Talked about everything. We played a game where we both had to ask each other ten questions. They had to be the same ten questions for both of us. And, we had to be totally honest. Kathy started."

"Are you married?"

"Yes."

"Children?"

"Yes, two. Boy aged four and a girl who's eighteen months."

"Are you happy?"

"Yes."

"Where do you live?"

"Surrey."

"House or flat?"

"House."

"Do you have any brothers or sisters?"

"A brother. Older. He lives in Canada."

"How old are you?"

"Thirty two."

"Are your parents alive?"

"Yes. Mum is fifty eight and dad is fifty nine."

"Do you love me?"

"Yes."

"Will you help me with something?"

"Yes."

"That was my ten questions done. Now it was Kathy's turn. We sat on the bed holding hands. I asked her the same ten questions. She wasn't married, she had no children, she wasn't happy but said she pretended to be. She lived in a bedsit in

Islington. She had no brothers or sisters and her parents were alive but living in Lincolnshire. She was twenty seven. She said she loved me and would help me. We almost drank the mini bar dry. We fell asleep fully clothed on the bed. We never had sex. Just held each other close. The next morning I walked her to the station and we swapped numbers. I wasn't sure if I would ever see her again. I got the train home knowing that I was in serious trouble. I'd been out all night, I hadn't called my wife. She would be angry but she would also be worried. I came up with a story. I'd met up with an old mate from school purely by chance when I was between appointments. He'd convinced me to take the afternoon off and go on a bender. I ended up sleeping on his couch absolutely legless. Bless her, she believed every word. She was just so relieved to see me. I took the rest of the day off, called in sick."

The big man leaned forward in his chair.

"So when did you see her again?"

Jim closed his eyes as though he was picturing the scene.

"It was three days later. A Friday, I think. She rang me. I was back in London. I was so relieved to hear her voice again. I thought she would never call. She asked if we could meet up again that day. I suggested Dirty Dicks, opposite Liverpool Street Station at four. Before she hung up she told me she loved me. I couldn't concentrate for the rest of the day. My heart was pounding like a bass drum. I finished my last meeting early. I could see it was going nowhere so just stood up and said that I didn't think our products were right for their company and walked out. I was at the pub by twenty past three. I walked in. She was already there. God she looked beautiful. Her blonde hair was tied back in a ponytail, she was wearing a tee shirt and jeans. Once again her pale skin looked luminous in the half light of the pub. I wanted her. She started giggling as I walked towards her."

"I've missed you Mr stationary man."

"I got us a bottle of wine and we found ourselves a quiet corner. I remember the sun was shining that day. It was quite hot so everyone was standing outside. The inside of the pub was practically empty. She asked me if I got in trouble for staying out all night. She held my hand as she spoke. Her big blue eyes looked so apologetic. I told her it was all fine and not to worry. Then came that lovely giggle of hers.

"It was fun though wasn't it?"

"I had to agree. She squeezed my hand tightly, then leaned across the table and kissed me softly on the lips. She tasted wonderful. We finished our wine and I made the mistake of looking at my watch. She noticed and asked me if I had to leave. I told her no and asked if she wanted more wine. She asked if I meant what I'd said in the Hotel Room about doing something for her. I smiled, at that moment I would have walked to the ends of the earth for her. She changed the subject and asked for another glass of wine. I went to the bar and got us two large glasses. When I returned to the table, she'd gone. She'd written something on a napkin."

"I'll call you in a few days to explain. Love you, mister paperclip."

The larger man put down his pen and paper and looked across at Jim. He'd stopped talking and there was an intense silence. His eyes were still closed.

"Jim, come on, let's carry on."

His eyes opened. The larger man noticed tears were rolling down his cheeks.

Jim stood up and shouted.

"I did what you wanted Kathy. I kept my promise!"

The larger man decided it was time for a break. He left the room and returned a few minutes later with two cups of black coffee.

"Jim, drink this. Then we must get on."

Jim took a sip of his coffee, wiped his eyes and continued.

"Where was I, oh yeh, the napkin. I've still got that napkin after all these years. Keep it in my desk at work. Look at it every day."

His eyes began to well up and his bottom lip began to tremble. The larger man brought him back to reality with kick to his shin.

"Jim, focus please, what happened next, after she left you in the pub?"

Suddenly Jim's whole persona changed. It was like a switch had been turned on and he was back to normal. Poised and composed.

"I was disappointed that she'd left so suddenly, but I suppose I loved her unpredictability. The next time she called was a week later. Again we arranged to meet in Dirty Dicks, in fact that place became a regular meeting place for us for the rest of that year. We met there once a week. We'd talk, drink wine, have a kiss and then she'd leave. We still hadn't had sex. I think for both of us we wanted it to be special. We wanted to take our time. We didn't want it to be some quickie somewhere. Every time we met she always asked me the same question just before we parted."

"Would you do anything for me Jim?"

"I always gave the same answer. Of course I would. I thought it was just a game that she loved to play. A game that proved to her how much I loved her. Then sometime in 2015, March I think, we met up as usual. She looked worried about something. I asked her if there was something wrong. She smiled but it was a reluctant smile."

"I'm fine Jim. Can you get away for a weekend?"

"I told her it might take some planning, but there was nothing I wanted more. She said her family had a small holiday cottage in Whitstable that they hardly ever used and she was going to move in there at the beginning of May. We kissed, finished our drinks and she left."

Jim looked at the large man. It was a look that said "Enough"?

The bigger man smiled.

"That's great so far Jim. Almost done here. Tell me how you managed to get a weekend away from the wife?"

"I began to sow the seeds indoors. I mentioned about a Sales Conference being planned for some time in May. Then I pretended to be angry that the company was planning it for a weekend. Then I wrote myself a letter on company headed paper and sent it to my home address. It confirmed that my presence was required at the Sales Conference in May. I had to be there on the Friday night and would return Sunday afternoon. My poor wife believed every word. As the date approached Kathy became more and more excited. Then it was time. I met her at the cottage at seven o'clock on the Friday evening. We took our time. Both of us didn't want to rush. I did some shopping on the way there and got us food and wine. I cooked. She loved the fact that I was making a fuss of her. The cottage had no television so there were no distractions. Just the two of us. She stood up suddenly, took my hand and led me to the bedroom. She asked me to undress her. I did. Slowly. As I took off each layer of clothing, I kissed her skin. She tasted wonderful. When she was naked her skin was milk bottle white. I told her she was the most beautiful thing I had ever seen. She smiled at me and lay down on the bed. I undressed and lay beside her. We didn't have sex. Sex doesn't describe what we had that night, nor does making love. It was more, much more than that. There was something else, something words can't describe. Intenseness, almost like our bodies had become one. It was the best night of my life. In fact that first weekend was something that will live with me forever, even when I'm gone. We stayed in the cottage for the remainder of that weekend. I've never felt so close to another human being in all my life. I didn't want it end. But sadly it had to. Just as I was getting ready to leave. She asked me a question.

"Will you keep me safe?"

"It was a strange question. But I answered it honestly. Always. I left on the Sunday afternoon. Not really wanting to. She waived me goodbye. We both had tears in our eyes. After that weekend I made regular trips to Whitstable. It was only an hour away and I would skive off work and go see her and still be home early evening. I started booking early appointments so that I could be finished by two in the afternoon and be in Whitstable by three. This went on for months. Then one day she told me."

"Jim. You know you always say you would do anything for me?"

"I gave my usual reply. Anything."

"Would you take someone's life for me?"

At first I thought she was joking. But her face told me she wasn't. I asked who? Her answer knocked me sideways."

"Me."

Jim fell silent, but the larger man knew he was close. Close to an answer.

"Jim, you say she asked you to kill her. I need to know why."

Jim sat forward and finished his coffee.

"She had an illness. A rare disease of the brain. One in ten million get it. She broke down as she told me that it could happen at any time. Her Doctor said she was lucky to still be alive. I was stunned. I didn't know what to say. I held her hand and asked how it would happen."

"I'll hallucinate, lose my memory. I won't know you Jim. You'll be a stranger to me. I couldn't bear that."

"I said there must be something someone could do, somewhere she could go for treatment. I offered to pay but she told me it was hopeless. Incurable, and that she'd accepted it now. We sat there in silence for what seemed like an age. Then she spoke."

"You promised Jim. You said you'd do anything. And if you don't do it I'll die and not remember you or our time together. You wouldn't want that for me, surely?"

"I tried to speak but she put her fingers to my lips to stop me then she kissed me on the cheek."

The larger man wanted just a bit more.

"So how did this "arrangement" happen then? Was there a time and place that you were supposed to do it?"

Jim was silent. He was staring at the ceiling.

"JIM, JIM, come on, we're close now. How and when did it happen?"

Jim turned his head and stared at the larger man.

"You do understand that I had to do it don't you. I promised."

The big man nodded.

"So you say. Now, how and when?"

"It was in Whitstable about a year later. She made me promise that as soon as she started to feel unwell it would be time. I went to see her one afternoon and she was acting strange. She didn't seem to know why she was there in the cottage. She thought she was being held prisoner. I knew then that I had to do it. She eventually calmed down and fell asleep. I stayed with her and lay by her side. When she woke up. She shouted.

"Get away, get away from me!"

"She thrashed about on the bed and I held her down until she went back to sleep. I took a pillow and held it down firm over her face. She didn't even struggle. I think that she knew what was happening and just let me get on with it. I kept me promise to her."

The larger man looked at Jim.

"And that's what happened was it Jim, you killed her because she was ill and she wanted you to?"

"I had to. I promised!"

The larger man put down his pen and paper and stood up. He walked around the desk and sat back down.

"That's a very interesting story Jim. Now let me tell you another story."

Jim's head had dropped. He was now staring at the floor.

"We spoke to your wife Jim. Lovely lady your wife. Did you know she keeps a diary?"

Now Jim looked up. He looked surprised.

"Yep Jim she writes in it every day. Do you know what she wrote on June 27th 2013?"

Jim looked back at the floor.

"She wrote. "Jim didn't come home tonight. Very worried. He's not answering his mobile." So that part of your story is correct Jim. But that's also the date that a twenty seven year old lady called Katherine Weller went missing. She was last seen in a café near Holborn. She was supposed to meet up with a group of friends at the Dirty Dick pub at Liverpool Street later that day, but never made it."

Jim didn't react. He just continued staring at the floor.

"Let's talk about Whitstable shall we Jim. You are registered as the leaseholder of a lock up railway arch there aren't you? We spoke to some of the other leaseholders. They say they've seen you coming and going over the past few years. They said that you were very secretive about the contents of the arch. You told one of them that you were restoring a classic car. Then last week, British Rail needed access to the arches. Seems there was a problem with the track above. They couldn't get hold of you Jim so had to force entry. Guess what they found in that old arch of yours Jim?"

For the first time Jim looked up. His face showed no emotion.

"Well the first thing they noticed was the smell. Horrible smell Jim. It was coming from a pit. You know the sort of pit that mechanics use so they can see the underneath of a car. Big pit it was. Five feet deep and about four feet square. Covered over with planks of wood. Guess what was inside that pit Jim?"

Jim started to shake his head.

"I promised to keep her safe, always."

"They found a chair, some rope and human remains Jim. That's what they found. We did some analysis Jim and discovered that they were the remains of a woman. A woman in her twenties. It was Katherine Weller Jim. Experts say that she died about three years ago. Which means that you kept her there alive in that pit for about two years? Visiting twice a week, probably giving her food and water, just enough to keep her alive. It's difficult to determine the cause of death after all this time Jim. Perhaps you can tell me."

"I promised to keep her safe, always. Then she started shouting. It was the illness. She thought she was being held prisoner. That's what the illness does it makes you hallucinate. She told me that, she said it would."

"Shall I tell you what I think Jim? I think that after she been in that pit for a while, she realised that she was never going to be released, so she asked you to kill her, get it over with. She must have been in so much agony that every time you visited her she would plead with you to end it. Then one day, maybe she struggled, shouted and you decided to give her what she wanted. So you killed her. Am I close Jim?"

"She told me, no, begged me to do it. You see, she was in pain. It was the illness you see. The illness."

The larger man pressed a button under the desk and two officers entered the room.

"Okay, we're done here for now. Take him back."

They grabbed Jim by his arms and lifted him from his chair. Just as they were about to leave the larger man called out.

"Just one more thing Jim. Are there any others? Any other young ladies that have asked for your help?"

Jim turned round to face the larger man. He was thinking.

"Three."

Leave The Lights On

Two Letters.

Jenny,

It's me. Please keep reading and don't tear this letter up. I beg
you.

Twelve years is a long time and I'm sorry. Sorry for so many
things.

Sorry for leaving you the way I did. No note, no reason, just left.
I was in a bad way back then and I knew that eventually I would
drag you down with me. The signs were there already. I used
every day and you were starting to do the same, and you with
our boy on the way. Not good.

 But not your fault, it was me that encouraged it. Without me I
knew you could stop. But if I stayed I was certain you'd lose
everything and I just couldn't bear that.

Sorry for missing our boys entry into this world and not being
there when times were hard for both of you. I don't even know
what you called him.

Sorry for missing his birthdays, his first day at nursery and
school. His first steps and words. Sorry.

Sorry for making you cry. You were the one that cried at every
soppy film we ever watched together, so I can imagine how
many tears you wept in those weeks and months after I left.

Sorry for not getting in touch during these past years. I just
couldn't, not until I was sure that all the scars had healed. It's
taken a long time for me to get myself straight and now,
eventually, I think I have. I'm clean. Have been for the past two
years. The journey's been a strange one. I've lived on the

streets, in squats, shelters and prison. I've begged, stolen and mugged. I found god once and then lost him again somewhere on the A13 near Whitechapel.

Sorry for taking the money out of the tin. I left with nothing but the clothes I had on. I had no idea where I was going or how I'd get there. The tin in the food cupboard had exactly seven pounds and thirty six pence in it. I took it for bus fare. Two pounds of it got me as far as Canning Town. Then I spent the rest on half a bottle of scotch. The next day I hitch hiked all the way to Hammersmith. I slept under the flyover for more than a year.

Sorry for all the shit you must have taken from your family. I knew they didn't like me, that was obvious. They must have seen us as we really were back then. A couple of fucked up junkies. Me, the instigator of everything and you being pulled along with blinkers on. I can only imagine how many times your Mum and dad said "You're better off without him." That must have been hell for you.

There are a million other things that I'm sorry for and I'd like to tell you face to face.

I'm close Jen. Real close. By the time you read this letter I'll be almost there. You may hate me and that's fine. But if there's a chance...even a slim one. Then I'll take it.

Even if it's just to say hello and give my boy a hug. Then that's also fine.

Jen, remember when we first met and I would go out with the lads and say I'd be home late?

Remember what you always said to me? About leaving the lights on?

So, give me a clue. Leave the light on in the front room. If it's on. I'll knock. If not I'll just walk away. Either way, I'll understand.

One thing has kept me going through these twelve years. The thought of one day getting back to you and our boy.

Please Jen, leave the light on.

Rob.

And here's the reply...

Dear Robert,

Your letter was forwarded onto me by the new tenants of Jenny's old flat.

I have read it and notice that you say "sorry" eleven times. Thank you for that.

Jenny's father and I are also sorry.

Sorry that we had to watch her fall apart after you left, just six weeks before the baby was due.

Sorry that we had to console her night after night because of her panic attacks and the relentless paranoia that she suffered from. You were right about the crying. She never stopped.

Sorry that we had to call for an ambulance when she tried to take her own life by overdosing on the stuff you left behind.

Sorry that our beautiful grandson was called a "crack baby" and only survived three days after the birth. We called him Steven. The name Robert was never even up for discussion.

Sorry that you had such a hard time living rough. Jenny also had a bit of a rough time. After Steven died she became withdrawn and had to receive professional help. She spent a year in a Psychiatric Hospital and was forever dependant on medication. We visited her every day.

We're also sorry that you couldn't find the time to write or call her just to let her know that you were okay. She would have loved that. In the end she was convinced that you were dead and when that happened she just couldn't bear to carry on. Jenny passed away eleven months ago. We thought she was over it, but she hid her illness well. The Police contacted us just after eleven o'clock on a Sunday morning. I won't go into detail, but the Thames can be very cold in February.

You mention us in your letter and you are right. We always thought she could do better than you. But you were her choice and we would have done what we could to see you both through your addiction. In fact on the day you left we were coming over to try to convince you to get help. We would have paid for any treatment you needed, but I suppose you had better ideas.

On the plus side, the letter you sent has answered one question that always troubled us. For ten years her electricity bill at the flat was enormous. Now we know why she kept every light on in the house twenty four hours a day.
Goodbye Robert.

Welcome To England

She stood there. Hands by her side. Back straight. Trying to look taller than her five feet seven inches. She'd been told to impress.

A tall bearded man was circling her just a few feet away. He shouted.

"Smile for fucks sake. Let's see those teeth!"

She did as she was told, put on a false smile then opened her mouth wide.

"Take off your top. "

Like a trained dog she obeyed him in an instant. She threw her blouse to the ground.

"And your bra!"

She unhooked it and let it slide to the floor. She stood there topless. Her body started to shiver from the cold night air.

The bearded man turned away from her and spoke to a shadowy figure in the corner of the damp railway arch.

"Is she clean?"

The man answered.

"Well, she's travelled in the back of a van for the past thirty six hours so I suppose she could do with a bit of a wash…"

"Don't fuck about Carlos. Is she CLEAN? Any infections, diseases, marks, cuts, bruises?"

"She's clean!"

"What is she?"

"Albanian."

"How old?"

"Eighteen? Maybe twenty?"

"Has she been used much?"

"Just a few times on the way over, that's all."

The bearded man ran his hands over her shoulders, arms, waist and legs. He poked a finger into her stomach.

"She's a bit skinny."

Carlos appeared from the shadows. A short, stocky, balding man in a leather jacket who appeared to have no neck.

"That's how everyone wants them these days. But she's got great tits. Anyway, she'll soon fatten up after a few takeaways."

The bearded man stroked his chin.

"How much?"

"Five thousand."

"Euros?"

Carlos laughed.

"Fuck off. Pounds!"

The bearded man shook his head.

"That's expensive."

"Bollocks, she'll earn you that and more in six months. If not just sell her on. You'll get three grand for her even if she's damaged."

The bearded man reached into his coat pocket, pulled out a bundle of fifty pound notes and handed them to Carlos.

"Okay. I'll take her."

Carlos took the money and smiled.

"She's yours. I've got a few more coming in next month from Nigeria. Interested?"

"You know me Carlos, if the price is right and they're in good nick them I'll take them. Give me a call when they arrive."

The two men shook hands and Carlos left.

The bearded man looked at the young girl in front of him.

"You speak English?"

Nervously the girl spoke.

"Yes, but not too good."

"Okay. Listen to me carefully, I just bought you, so you belong to me now. Understand?"

The girl nodded. The bearded man put his face close to hers.

"You call me boss. Okay?"

Again the girl nodded.

The bearded man slapped her hard across the face, causing her head to jerk violently to the right. She stumbled but quickly regained her position and stood up straight. Again the man leaned in close so that his face was only inches from hers.

"I said, you call me boss. Okay?"

"Yes boss."

"That's better. Now put your fucking clothes on and come with me."

She sat quietly in the back of the old Volvo estate while the bearded man drove slowly through the brightly lit streets.

After thirty minutes the car stopped outside a terraced house in a quiet street.

The bearded man got out and opened her door. He clapped his hands.

"Come on, chop chop."

Hurriedly she slid along the back seat and almost fell out of the car. The man had already started walking up the pathway of one of the houses. She closed the car door and ran quickly to catch him up.

The door was opened by a woman in her late forties with a complexion that gave away her sixty a day smoking habit. Without saying a word the bearded man turned and walked back down the path. Leaving the girl unsure of what to do next.

The woman grabbed her arm and pulled her roughly into the house. She looked the girl up and down as though she was trying to guess her worth. She spoke in a broad London accent.

"You speak English?"

The girl nodded.

"A little."

"Good. What's your name?"

"Ardita. My name is Ardita."

The woman put her hands on her hips.

"Where you from?"

"Berat. It's a small town in Albania."

The woman let out a sigh.

"To be honest I really don't give a shit where you're from. But for what it's worth, welcome to fucking England."

Me, Dad And Ali

"For as long as I can remember he was always there in the background."

I first became aware of the name Cassius Clay in 1963. I was five years old. Dad said that some cocky black kid was coming over to fight "Our Enry".

Dad was a big fan of Henry Cooper. But knew his limitations. He'd watched him come up through the amateurs and then turn professional. He always said that Cooper was a good British champion but was never world class. He said many times "Those yanks are just too big and strong for Henry."

But, he was convinced that the kid who'd won the Olympic Gold medal just a couple of years before would be no match for our man. Dad let me stay up that night and we listened to the fight on the radio. Cooper put Clay on the floor with a great left hook in round three but Clay survived and two rounds later the referee was stopping the fight to save poor Henry's face from suffering further damage. I saw the photos in the paper the next day. I wondered how a man could lose so much blood yet still live.

A month after my sixth birthday dad tells me that the cocky black kid is going to fight Sonny Liston for the world title. He laughs. "He won't last more than a couple of rounds with the Bear." The Big Bear was Liston's nickname. I didn't know why at the time but anyone who was called a Bear MUST be big, strong and as hard as nails. The next morning, I wake up and go downstairs to find dad reading the paper. He looks at me and shakes his head. "He's only gone and beaten the Bear! I can't believe it! He's beaten the Bear!" I stood there in my Batman Pyjamas and started shaking MY head as well. I couldn't believe it either.

Me and Dad had to wait over a year before the black kid fought again. This time in a rematch with Sonny Liston. At seven years of age I sat glued to the radio to listen to the commentary in the early hours of the morning. Clay beat Liston in the first round. I remember Dad getting to his feet and saying "This can't be right. It's a fix, it must be. No one beats Liston in one round!"

A few days later and dad tells me that Cassius Clay now wants be called Muhammed Ali. I ask why. "It's a religious thing" he says. Then he laughs. "Or some kinda gimmick to sell more tickets for his next fight. Makes no difference, he'll always be known as Cassius Clay."

Six months later and he beats another one of Dad's favourite fighters. Floyd Patterson. Dad's impressed. "Well, if he can beat Liston and Patterson, the kid must be something special." He tells me this as he applies a giant handful of Brylcreem to his hair then carefully combs it through to get the perfect quiff.

In 1966 we're all getting excited about the World Cup finals right here in London. But there was another reason to be excited. Cassius Clay was coming to London for two fights. First against Henry Cooper at Arsenal's Football Ground and then against Brian London at Earls Court. Both fights would be shown live on TV. For the first time we'd get to see for ourselves just how good this kid was.

We were both convinced there could only be one outcome. Clay would beat them both. We were right.

Cooper lasted till round six before the referee stopped the fight because of another bad cut eye. Eleven weeks later and just one week after England beat West Germany to win the world cup, Clay steps into the ring to face Brian London. That night me and dad sat round the television at my Aunty Flo's house in Stamford Hill in North London. Never have I seen a more one sided fight. London looked a beaten man even before he entered the ring. It was like watching the skinny kid in class being asked to scrap with the best fighter in the school. Somehow he knows he has to turn up to save face but he always knows he's going to get hurt. In the third round Clay threw twelve punches in three seconds. ALL of them hit London hard. The ref counted him out.

Just five weeks later and we were watching him step into the ring again. This time in Germany against a big guy called Karl Mildenberger. Clay beat him in twelve rounds.

Dad had never seen anyone like him before and with my limited knowledge of the noble art neither had I. I'd watched old footage of Joe Louis, Rocky Marciano, Max Baer and Jack Johnson. All great Heavyweights in their time but none of them were this quick. None of them danced around the ring with such elegance and style. None of them could bob, weave, sway and avoid being hit like Clay.

After these three wins in Europe Clay returned to American and defended his World title three times in just four months. We listened to all of them on the radio in the middle of the night. Of course, he won them all.

I notice something change in Dad. He no longer refers to the cocky black kid as Cassius Clay. He now calls him Ali. So from that time onwards, so do I.

At just nine years of age, I have two heroes. My dad and a big cocky black man who just happens to be the Heavyweight Champion of the World.

But, everything was about to change.

I came home from school and sat down to eat corn beef, chips and pickle. I started gulping it down as fast as I could because Animal Magic was about to start on the TV. Mum wanted to know what I'd done at school that day and I mumbled something about Maths and PE. Then she told me the news.

"You know that boxer that you and Dad like? Well he's refused to go in the army and so he's no longer the World Champion. He might even go to prison."

She said it in a very matter of fact way while she was scrubbing one of dad's shirts at the sink.

I stopped chewing a mouthful of chips and pickle and sat bolt upright. Animal Magic no longer seemed important. The News would be on in an hour and Dad would be home from work at six. He'd know for sure what was going on. I was hoping that somehow mum had got it all wrong.

Sixty minutes later and I'm watching the news in disbelief. Ali was refusing to fight for his country. People were calling him a coward.

I heard the front door shut and dad came rushing into the front room. He looked at me and then the TV.

"Is it true? He's been stripped of his title for refusing to go to Vietnam?"

I just nodded. Even though I had no idea what or where Vietnam was.

"He can't be a coward dad can he? He fought Sonny Liston twice and beat him easily, and he's The Big Bear! He can't be a coward, not Ali."

Dad came and sat next to me on the floor.

"No he's not a coward. But, when you're asked to fight for your country you have to do it."

I said what most nine year olds would say. "Why?"

Dad just shrugged his shoulders.

"Cos that's the rules. It's just the way things are."

He stood up and walked into the kitchen. He gave mum a kiss then went to the sink to wash his hands and face before having his tea. He took off his jumper and shirt and stood there in his old white vest. He took a bar of Lifebuoy soap and begun to scrub his hands. As he did so he turned his head and spoke to me over his shoulder.

"The yanks are in a war with the Vietnamese, they want everyone to do their bit to fight the communists."

I had no idea what any of that meant, but we had a set of old Encyclopaedias piled up beside the piano. Mum had paid a shilling for them at a jumble sale a year before and almost gave herself a hernia carrying them home. She said they would come in handy. But after twelve months they were still exactly where she'd left them and no one had taken any notice of them. Until now.

I was desperate to find out why my hero wouldn't fight for his country. I flicked through the pages and read everything I could on words I'd heard on the news and from Dad. I found out where Vietnam was, I read about the US Draft system, I even read about Communism. At just nine years old I became fascinated with the Vietnam war and why America had become involved.

Ali never went to prison. But his boxing licence was taken away as was his passport. No one knew how long it would be before he got them back.

With Ali no longer holding the World Boxing Association title, it was decided that there should be an eight-man tournament to decide who should be the next Champion Of The World. Dad thought this was a farce.

"It's nonsense. Ali's already beaten four of them and the other four wouldn't last more than a couple of rounds with him."

Jimmy Ellis beat Jerry Quarry in the final and became World Heavyweight Champion.

But me and dad had lost interest. No longer would we stay up till silly o'clock in the morning to listen to the fights. There was no excitement, no anticipation, no flair, no Ali.

The rest of 1967 came and went as did 1968 and 1969. I left junior school and at the age of eleven and started at the local Comprehensive. Dad left Fords Motor Company and started with the local Gas works. We moved from a tiny two-bedroom council house to a much bigger three-bedroom council house on the other side of town.

Jimmy Ellis defended his title just once, against an aging Floyd Patterson. He won on points. Boring.

But there was a new kid on the block. Joe Frazier. He'd had ten fights since Ali was stripped of his title and won them all. He was recognised as the World Champion by another organisation, the NYSAC. It was announced that he would fight Jimmy Ellis at Madison Square Gardens in February 1970. For the first time in almost three years me and dad wanted to see who would win and become the undisputed world champion. Although we knew very little about Joe Frazier we were convinced he would batter Ellis within a few rounds.

Dad woke me up at 2am and we went downstairs and turned on the radiogram. Dad made tea and toast and we sat down to listen to the commentary. Frazier knocked Ellis down twice in the fourth round and his trainer refused to let him come out for the fifth to save him further punishment. We looked at each other and agreed. At last we had a worthy Heavyweight Champion. He was good, but he still wasn't Ali.

The world was changing and so were attitudes. Especially in America. The war in Vietnam had become extremely unpopular. People were beginning to wonder what the hell they were doing sending their sons and loved ones to fight a war thousands of miles away. The same people who had once branded Ali a coward now had sympathy and understanding for his stand. He spoke at rallies and colleges across the US telling anyone who would listen about civil rights.

And then it happened.

In August 1970 we were on holiday in Dovercourt, a small seaside town in Kent. My Aunt Rose had a caravan there and said we could have it for a week. We had a routine. Mum and my sister would cook the breakfast while me and dad went to fill up the water bottles and get the morning paper. I stood outside the paper shop while dad went inside. When he came out he looked at me and raised his arms in the air and shouted.

"He's got his licence back! He's fighting Jerry Quarry in two months' time!"

A thirty-nine-year-old man and a twelve-year-old boy began to dance in the street.

This was turning out to be the best holiday of all time.

The night of October 26th 1970 would be a long one. Instead of going to bed early and getting up at 2am, me and dad decided to stay up and keep awake with lots of tea and biscuits. Dad managed it but I fell asleep around midnight. He woke me just after 2.30am. But, there was a problem. No matter how hard we tried we just couldn't find the commentary anywhere on the radio. We thought we'd found it once but the reception was so bad that we couldn't understand a word that was being said. I joked with dad that it was like listening to the Clangers. Disappointed but undeterred, we stayed up all night and waited for the result to come through. It came on the 5am news.

Ali beat Jerry Quarry in three rounds. The referee stopped the fight due to a bad cut around Quarry's left eye. The report said that Ali dominated the fight with his left jab and moved well around the ring. But the report also added that Ali was slower and heavier than he had been almost four years earlier. Dad was outraged.

"Of course he's slower. He nearly thirty now, he's been out of the ring for four years, you've got to expect him to be different. But, I bet you he's still got what it takes to get his title back."

I of course agreed with every word.

Less than two months later and he was back in the ring again, this time against the rugged Argentinian fighter Oscar Bonavena. Me and dad had a bet. He said it wouldn't last seven rounds. I said Ali would win in round 10. The prize would be a Mars Bar. We were both wrong. The referee stopped the fight in the fifteenth and final round after Bonavena had been knocked down three times. It hadn't been an easy fight as a lot of people had predicted, but Ai had won and was now a real title contender. Dad bought a Mars Bar and we had half each...

The news we'd been waiting for came a few weeks later. Ali would face Joe Frazier at Madison Square Gardens on Monday 8th March for the Undisputed Heavyweight Championship of the World.

Mum had a calendar hanging on the wall in the kitchen. Dad put a big circle around the fight date and every day after school I would go straight to the calendar and mark off another day.

Dad did the football pools every week and each time he filled out his coupon he would say the same thing.

"If I win the pools son. We're going to New York and we'll get the best seats in the house!"

On Saturday afternoons we'd sit and watch the results come in at five o'clock on BBC Grandstand. Both with our fingers crossed hoping to win the Jackpot. While this was going on mum would be cooking our "Cowboy" tea. Egg, Bacon and beans.

Dad never did win the pools so we settled for listening to it on the radio instead. Didn't matter. All that mattered was that Ali won the fight and got his title back.

Finally, the big day came, and this time we were prepared. The radiogram was tuned into the right station and just in case it broke down we had a transistor radio on standby. Mum went to bed around eleven and me and dad looked forward to the long night ahead. Just after midnight dad gave me a wink and went into the kitchen. He came back with a bottle of Cherryade and the biggest bowl of sweets I'd ever seen! Liquorice Allsorts, Merry Maid Toffees, Sherbet Bonbons and my absolute favourite. A whole bar of Coconut Ice!

The sugar rush should have killed us both, instead it just made us even more excited than we were already. Shortly after, the coverage began.

The commentator said that there were celebrities everywhere. Frank Sinatra, Burt Lancaster and Kirk Douglas were all there and ringside tickets were going for two hundred dollars each. I had no idea how much that was in real money but dad said it was a small fortune!

The bell rang and the fight started.

Ali was quick in the first few rounds, jabbing and moving just like the old days. But we both knew he couldn't keep it up for too long. At the end of round three the unthinkable happened. Frazier landed a massive left hook and Ali was visibly shaken but didn't go down. Frazier won the next few rounds and was now ahead on points. Me and Dad were convinced that Ali was just taking it easy so that he could come on strong in the final rounds and might even knock out Frazier towards the end of the fight. But it didn't happen. It was Frazier who finished the strongest. Despite Ali doing well in the thirteenth and fourteenth, Frazier was still standing and ahead on all three scorecards. The bell rang for the fifteenth and then the impossible really did happened. Smoking Joe caught Ali with a punch that would have floored a rhino and Ali went down. Just for three seconds but he was down. I had my head in my hands and when I looked up so did dad. And then it was over. The bell rang to signal the end of the fight. Ali had lost by a unanimous decision.

We sat there in silence. The commentator was saying that after this defeat Ali should retire.

Dad could see that I was close to tears. He put his arm around me.

"They're talking nonsense. Retire? Ali? Are they mad? He's been fighting all his life for what he believes in. He's not going to let one defeat get in his way. He'll be back. You mark my words. He'll be back and he'll be even better that he was before!"

Instead of going to bed miserable and disappointed, dad's words made sense and cheered me up. Ali would be back. I was sure of it.

Ali didn't retire. Instead he had three more fights in 1971, winning them all. Including the man that held the title in his absence, Jimmy Ellis. Joe Frazier on the other hand didn't fight again that year, some say because the Ali fight had taken so much out of him.

Along came 1972 and all our lives changed.

I was fourteen and started going out with girls. A date would usually consist of going to "The Pictures" or the local Wimpy Bar. I started drinking beer, (dad knew but mum didn't) and I got my first job. A Saturday boy at a local Butchers shop. I did all day Saturday and helped them clear up three nights a week after school. I got paid £10 and took home a bag full of meat for the rest of the family. I was growing up fast.

Dad was made redundant from the local Gas works and got a job as a delivery driver for a local office furniture store. He loved it. No more shift work meant he left the house at seven thirty and was back sitting down to have tea with the rest of us at five o'clock.

Ali was on his second marriage and in 1972 his fourth child was born. Muhammad Ali Jnr. He also starred in his first film, Black Rodeo, where he rode a horse down 125th street in Harlem.

But the one thing that was constant was Boxing.

While Joe Frazier, the World Champion, only had two easy fights, Ali was fighting everyone they put in front of him. He fought in Canada, Japan, America and even came to Ireland to fight Alvin Lewis. He had seven fights in ten months and won them all. He had to beat one more contender then he would be ranked as the number one challenger. Everything looked set for a rematch with Frazier.

All Ali had to do was beat a guy called Ken Norton and all Frazier had to do was defend his title against George Foreman. Then the fight we'd all been waiting for could be set up for early 1973. Easy!

We had a New Year's Eve Party to see out 1972 and welcome in 1973. Family, friends and neighbours were all invited. We must have had over forty people in our little council house and whilst the girls were dancing to Son Of My Father by Chicory Tip, the men were in the kitchen drinking beer and talking about boxing. Me included. I was just a few weeks away from my fifteenth birthday and dad let me have a few beers. There was cans of Party Seven scattered everywhere.

Everyone was convinced that Frazier would beat Foreman. Except dad.

"Frazier has been lazy for the past year. He's only fought twice and that was against nobodies. Foreman is knocking everyone out. I know people are saying that he's yet to meet anyone of Frazier's standard, but he's not just beating these guys, he's destroying them. I think he'll beat Frazier."

For the first time EVER I couldn't agree with dad.

"But Frazier beat Ali. He must beat Foreman!"

For the next hour, cheese and pineapple was eaten, beer was drunk, and the fight was discussed in depth. All through the haze of thick cigarette smoke.

At three o'clock in the morning I went to bed with the sound of Aunty Hilda singing Long Haired Lover from Liverpool at the top of her voice, accompanied by Uncle Vic on the spoons and Dad on the piano.

The Frazier V Foreman fight was just a few days before my fifteenth birthday. It was taking place in Kingston, Jamaica. Me and Dad did our usual and got ourselves comfortable in the front room. But times had changed. No more Cherryade and sweets, this time it was a few cans of Skol lager and crisps and peanuts. No more bets for Mars Bars, this time it was for a crisp five-pound note.

Dad won the fiver (though he never took it). Foremen destroyed Frazier in just two rounds. The referee stopped the fight after Frazier had been down for the SIXTH time.

Foreman was now being described as the most dangerous fighter on the planet. If Ali was to going to get his title back, he would have to fight the "beast" that was George Foreman.

Two months later and Ali is fighting Ken Norton in San Diego California. Me and Dad listen in disbelief as the fight goes the distance and Norton is declared the winner. When we read the headlines the next day we discover that in the early rounds Ali suffered an injury and fought most of the fight with a broken jaw. Once again people were talking about Ali retiring. One of the boxing journalists wrote "He's thirty-one and the road back to the World title is going to be a long and hard one. He'll have to fight Norton again, then probably Frazier before he can get to Foreman. And to be honest that's a fight that he is unlikely to win."

For the first time in my life I began to think that maybe, just maybe, it was the end of the road.

Dad on the other hand was adamant.

"I've said it before and I'll say it again. He'll come back. He always does."

Thankfully dad's crystal ball was working fine, because that's exactly what he did. He rested up for six months but came back and beat Norton in the rematch. Now for Frazier. We waited for the announcement.

I was sitting listening to Mum go on about how much she would miss Elsie Tanner in Coronation street when dad came home from work and walked into the kitchen. He just stood there looking at me with a massive grin on his face. I saw his grin and matched it with my own.

"What?"

He couldn't get the words out fast enough.

"It's on. The Frazier v Ali fight is on. And guess what date?"

I couldn't guess. I didn't know where this was going. So I just shrugged my shoulders.

"When?"

Dad said the words slowly.

"The..Twenty Eighth... of... January!"

My jaw actually dropped.

"My sixteenth Birthday!"

He put his arm around me and said the words I'll never forget.

"And we're going son. I'm taking you to see it!"

I heard him say the words but they didn't really sink in.

He sat down at the kitchen table.

"Look, the fight's in New York. Obviously we can't go to New York and even if we could we'd never be able to afford the price of the tickets. But, there's this new thing. Certain Cinemas around the country are going to show it live in the early hours of the morning. I've checked it out and East Ham Odeon is one of them. Tickets go on sale in a few days' time. We're going!"

To me, that was just as good as going to New York. I didn't know what to say. It seemed unreal. We were going to see Ali fight LIVE. Not just any old fight, but THE fight. Ali v Frazier 2.

I don't know how I got through the next few weeks but somehow I managed it. By the time my Birthday came I'd already left school and started full time in the Butchers shop learning the trade. My boss, Roy, enrolled me on a one day a week course at Butchery College in Smithfield.

Dad spent thirty-five pounds on two tickets for the fight. This was more than his weekly wage and I can only imagine what he and mum must have sacrificed to get them.

Fight day, and my birthday, was a Monday. That was my college day and I finished in London around 3pm. On the way home I stopped off at a record shop where my mate worked. I always asked him to save me any new Soul albums that were released. That day there were three. Bobby Womack, Blue Magic and Love Unlimited Orchestra. I was indoors by 4.30pm and I knew I had two hours before dad came home. Enough time to play the new albums in my bedroom and get ready for the night ahead. Headphones on, eyes shut and singing at the top of my voice! The next thing I knew mum was shaking me and saying dinner was ready. Dad was now home and we sat at the kitchen table for the next three hours discussing the fight. My Birthday tea (and dad's) was a massive piece of Rump steak and two eggs. Mum called it a dinner for Champions!

East Ham Odeon opened its doors at midnight and guess who were first in the queue.

Even though it was a non-title fight it was a sell-out. There was an undercard but to be honest no one was really watching it. Everyone just wanted to see the main event.

My boss from the Butchers shop, Roy, decided he wanted to come along and he bought a ticket from a tout outside. He was supposed to be seated a few rows behind us but he was the sort of bloke that you didn't argue with and instead got someone to move and took a seat next to me. No booze was allowed in the Cinema but Roy came in with a 2 litre bottle of Coke under his coat. Half of it was Bacardi!

Dad was no drinker but I decided it would be good of me to help Roy out by drinking as much as I could. It all added to the excitement.

Finally, everyone took their seats and we waited for the fighters to appear. There were a few cheers for Frazier but the place erupted as Ali stepped into the ring. He looked like a giant. He was four inches taller than Frazier and half a stone heavier. His reach was an impressive eighty-two inches, almost ten more than Frazier's. He was awesome.

And then it began.

Wow, Ali had completely changed his style of fighting. This was no quick jab and move around the ring. He threw a flurry of punches then grabbed Frazier around the head with one arm and held him tight in a clinch with the other. There was no way Frazier could punch him from close range. He won the first round. In round two he did the same and just before the bell caught Frazier with a great right hand. Everyone stood up thinking Frazier might just go down. But he didn't and Ali won that round as well. His new style wasn't pretty but it was working and Frazier was getting frustrated.

Me and dad were scoring every round on our programme. At the end of round six I asked dad what he thought.

"Four to Ali, one to Frazier and one even."

I agreed. Exactly the same as me.

The second half of the fight saw Frazier win a few more rounds but when the final bell came we both had Ali in front. It was close but I had him winning it by two rounds while dad thought only one.

When the announcement came the referee held up Ali's hand. He'd won it by a unanimous decision.

We left the stadium about 5am. I was exhausted and slightly drunk. But wow, what a night. Roy let me have the Tuesday morning off and I slept till midday. Dad didn't, he had a few cups of tea then went to work.

It was all I could talk about for weeks after. When people asked me what I did for my birthday I would go on and on about the fight telling them every detail. I must have bored the pants off everyone. But it wasn't just me. Dad was the same. We'd talk about it over tea most nights and discuss what Ali had to do to beat the "beast" George Foreman.

Both of us wanted Ali to get his title back, but we also realised that he would be up against the meanest fighter on the planet who just happened to have the hardest punch in boxing. Ali had beaten Frazier on points, Foreman had literally destroyed him in two rounds.

Without really saying it, we were both worried that he could be seriously hurt. It was a fight that he couldn't win. Or could he?

Two months later and George Foreman was defending his World title against Ken Norton. This was the man that broke Ali's jaw, took him the distance and beat him on points. Although Ali got his revenge in the rematch, it was a close fight and some thought Norton should have got the verdict.

Me and Dad did our usual and listened to the fight on the radio. I was convinced that Norton would put up a good show and last into the latter rounds. He was a big strong man with a granite chin who wouldn't go down easily. Dad wasn't so sure.

I was wrong. Foreman hit him so hard early in round two that Norton buckled and wobbled and tried to stay on his feet. But Forman kept on relentlessly and Norton went down twice before the referee decided to step in and stop it.

If me and dad were concerned about Ali before, now we were terrified. Foreman might just kill him.

Shortly afterwards it was announced that Ali would face Foreman in Kinshasa, Zaire on 25th September 1974. The papers were calling it "The Rumble In The Jungle." We couldn't wait, but we had to, it was three months away.

The summer came and in August I had my first holiday away without mum and dad. I had a mate whose parents had a caravan at Selsey on the Sussex coast. He was seventeen and had just passed his driving test. His dad got him an old MK1 Cortina and so five of us headed off on holiday. We broke down before we even got out of London. Luckily one of the lads was an apprentice at Fords and with the help of the belt from my jeans, some chewing gum and an elastic band managed to get us going again.

What my mate had failed to tell any of us was that his girlfriend had rented the caravan next door. Her and four of her mates! I paired up quickly with a girl called Lisa. She was a year older than me and from Lewisham. For a week we were like boyfriend and girlfriend. This was the summer of "Kung Fu Fighting and Rock Your Baby."

We spent most of the day in bed and in the evening we'd go out and drink and dance.

It was the best holiday I'd ever had. But when I got back dad had some bad news.

"It's off. The fights been put back a month. Foreman got a cut in sparring so they've set a new date for October 30th."

I didn't swear much at that time, especially not in front of mum and dad, but I just couldn't help it.

"Fuck, another month to wait."

It might have been a long wait for me and dad, but Ali used it to his advantage. He toured the whole of Zaire making himself popular with the people. Everywhere he went they chanted his name. Soon the whole of Zaire was rooting for him. He encouraged them to shout "Ali. Bomaye", which literally meant "Ali. Kill him."

Once again the fight would be shown live at selected cinemas and this time our nearest venue was in Ilford. I was working full time and was earning reasonable money, so I decided to surprise dad and came home one evening with two tickets. Not just any old tickets. I'd asked my boss for an advance and bought two tickets in the front row! Dad's face was a picture when I put them on the kitchen table. I think he was quite proud of his "little boy."

As usual we were at the cinema waiting for the doors to open. We took our seats and waited for the undercard to begin. Once again it was a sell out and the majority of the audience were Ali supporters, all wanting him to win, but not really expecting it to happen.

Reg Gutteridge, a journalist from the London News and, for me and dad, the BEST boxing commentator ever, was doing the talking. "Tonight Ali has promised to do something special. He says he has a secret weapon. Let's see what happens."

The bell rang and Ali came out jabbing with his right hand and not his left, something he'd never done before. This confused Foreman and Ali scored well in the first couple of minutes but by the end of the round Foreman had adapted well. So round one to Ali.

In round two Ali did something that had never been seen before in boxing, especially at Heavyweight. He leaned back against the ropes, put his head into his chest and covered up with his arms, then encouraged George to hit him! Was he mad? Okay so Foreman could only hit his body and his arms but the punches would surely break his ribs. Foreman hit him with everything he had for a full thirty seconds, then Ali came back with a flurry of punches and moved away. This went on for the next three rounds. Ali taking punch after punch from Foreman and then throwing three or four of his own. I looked at dad.

"What's he doing? Why is he letting Foreman hit him like that?"

Dad smiled.

"They're not really scoring punches and he's obviously trying to wear Foreman out. It's risky, but it might just work."

But Foreman dominated the fifth round. Throwing good solid accurate shots. But just before the bell rang Ali threw a number of punches that all landed cleanly and visibly shook Foreman, he looked tired when he went back to his corner.

Rounds six and seven saw Foreman throw more and more wild and desperate punches at Ali, most of them landing on arms and torso. Very few of them scoring points. Now Ali was taunting Foreman. Every time they were in a clinch you could hear him clearly saying "That all you got George?"

At the end of the seventh round Foreman went back to his corner looking a very tired man. Dad was on his feet.

"I think he's got him."

The bell sounded for round eight and Foreman came forward like he had in every round before, but his punches no longer had the same venom. He was an exhausted man. Then the thing that couldn't possibly happen, happened!

Foreman had Ali on the ropes once again and was throwing wild rugged punches. Ali moved away quickly and as he did so threw a five punch combination quickly followed by a left hook that lifted Foreman's head up only to be met with a crushing right hand from Ali. Foreman was off balance and exhausted. He crashed to the canvas.

He looked dazed and confused and rose to his feet at the count of nine. But too late, the referee had decided he'd had enough. It was over.

There was mayhem in the cinema. People were jumping up and down and shouting "Ali.Ali.Ali."

I turned and hugged dad just as I had as a little kid. A miracle had happened and we'd been there to witness it.

Even the commentator Reg Gutteridge couldn't believe it. As the referee counted Foreman out he shouted "Oh my god. He's won the title back at thirty-two!"

Me and dad were convinced that Ali would now retire as possibly the greatest Heavyweight the world had ever seen. There was no one left to beat. He'd dominated the Heavyweight division for a decade. We loved him and loved to see him fight but it was time to say goodbye.

But Ali had other plans....

1975 was a year of change for me, dad and Ali.

Ali changed his religion from The Nation Of Islam to mainstream Sunni Muslim.

Dad became a self-employed man at 44. He opened up his first seafood stall outside a pub in Essex.

Me? I changed from drinking Light and Bitter to Lager...

It was also the year The War in Vietnam ended. The North took the South and the Americans left. It seemed Ali was right all along.

As one war ended another one started. The UK was at war with Iceland. Over Cod!

The film Jaws was released and an American gangster called Jimmy Hoffa went missing.

Oh, and a certain lady called Margaret Thatcher became the leader of the Conservative party.

The one thing that remained the same was boxing. Ali kept fighting and me and dad kept watching.

He took five months off then had three fights in 1975. He won them all but didn't look that impressive. I was beginning to think that the gruelling fights with Frazier and Foreman had taken their toll.

Then the news came that he was to fight Joe Frazier for the third time. In the Philippines!

A date was set for 1st October 1975.

During the build-up Ali came up with a poem to sum up the fight. "It will be a killa and a thrilla and a chilla, when I get that Gorilla in Manilla."

The papers loved it and the fight became known as The Thrilla In Manilla.

Me and dad had a long discussion about the fight one night while mum was at bingo. I believed Ali would win easily.

"Frazier's only had two fights since Ali beat him eighteen months ago. He won them both but they were weak opponents. He's not the same fighter since Foreman destroyed him. I see Ali beating him in eight rounds."

Dad wasn't so optimistic.

"Yeh but look at Ali. He's had more fights but hasn't looked impressive since he beat Foreman. I think it goes the distance but Ali wins on points."

So we were both sure Ali would win, but not convinced that it would be a great fight.

Boy...were we wrong.

Another sell out at the cinema in Ilford. Dad had coconut ice and I had the sherbet bon bons. It was just like old days. As the Master Of Ceremonies introduced them, they both looked in great shape. Ali was taller and heavier that Frazier with a big reach advantage. But everyone knew that Frazier could hit and hit hard.

When they met in the centre of the ring for the referee's instructions you could hear Ali taunting Frazier.

"You aint got it no more Joe, I'm gonna put you away."

Frazier took no notice. He just smiled and as he walked back to his corner he muttered.

"We'll see."

The bell rang and they came out quickly. Frazier was always a notoriously slow starter and Ali jabbed away with his left, scoring good points. He then threw two or three right hands in quick succession and Frazier had no answer. Ali won the first two rounds easily. In the third he tried the tactic that had worked against Foreman, where he leaned against the ropes and encouraged his opponent to hit him, hoping he would tire. Now known as the Rope a dope. Frazier was ready for it and landed hard solid hurting punches to Ali's body. This continued for the next three rounds.

In the sixth Frazier caught Ali with a tremendous left hook, Ali slumped back on the ropes, he was hit with another left and looked like he might go down. But he didn't and the bell rang for the end of the round. Seven and eight were gruelling rounds for both fighters. Each throwing and landing big shots. At the end of the ninth Ali looked visibly tired as he walked back to his stool. He told his corner "Man this is the closest thing to dying!"

In the tenth and eleventh we watched as both men gave everything they had. Frazier's eyes were swelling and it was obvious that he was couldn't see some of the punches that Ali was throwing. Ali was tiring, he'd thrown hundreds of punches but Frazier just wouldn't go down. In the thirteenth and fourteenth round Ali piled on the pressure, hitting Frazier with everything he had. Punch after punch landed cleanly into Frazier face, but he just kept coming back. Before the bell rang for the start of the fifteenth it was obvious that Frazier couldn't continue. His trainer signalled to the referee to say his fighter wasn't coming out for the final round. Frazier was begging to let him continue. But the fight was over.

Once again me and dad had witnessed history being made. We'd just seen the greatest Heavyweight Boxing match the world had ever seen.

At home drinking tea at 6am before we both went to work having had no sleep, we were now sure that it was time for Ali to retire. He'd done it. He'd "Shook up the world." Just like he said he would all those years ago. There was no one left to beat. He was without doubt "The Greatest." and had nothing more to prove.

We just prayed that he agreed...

Surprise, surprise. Ali didn't retire. Three months later he defended his title against a little known Belgium fighter called Jean – Pierre Coopman. Ali knocked him out in the fifth round. He had four fights in 1976 and two in 1977. He won them all and of course, me and dad were there at the cinema to watch him do it.

Ali had transcended boxing. He was the most recognised man on the planet. I'm sure if you found a long lost tribe somewhere in the remote Amazon rainforest and showed them his photo, they would have smiled and said "Ali."

In those two years, I had my first holiday abroad, passed not only my driving test but also my Butchery exams and became a "Master Butcher". I was no longer working for my boss Roy. He had gone off to pastures new and I was renting the shop from him. At nineteen, I was running my own business. And I was still drinking Lager....

Dad continued with the fish stall and was working hard. Mum helped out by boiling live crabs in the kitchen and working on the stall at weekends.

Dad was driving a Ford Corsair and I was driving an Austin Cambridge. Ali could have had any car he wanted.

On 15th February 1978 we went to see Ali fight a little known boxer called Leon Spinks. Me and Dad had never heard of him and thought Ali would despatch him in just a few rounds.

We sat there in disbelief as we watched this young kid take on an out of shape Ali and beat him. When the fight ended after fifteen rounds we were both convinced that Spinks had done enough to win. We were right. Ali had lost his title.

The question now was, not just WOULD he come back, but COULD he?

The answer was obvious really. The world wanted the rematch and would pay good money to see it. Leon Spinks knew that no other fighter in the world could give him the payday that he wanted. So the rematch was arranged for the 15th September 1978. It took place in New Orleans and broke all box office and attendance records.

In the space of the two fights I got engaged to a girl from East Ham. We set the wedding day for March 1979.

Ali got himself in shape but the fight was disappointing. At the end of fifteen rounds Ali was easily the winner. He won by a unanimous decision. He was the first man ever to win the Heavyweight title three times. That was it. He'd once again done the impossible. Now surely he would retire.

Ali took his time deciding, but in July 1979 came the announcement we'd expected. Muhammad Ali had retired from boxing.

Me and dad gave a sigh of relief. It was time. He'd done everything, beat everyone and won every title there was. His body had suffered enough. They were great fights to watch but they were life threatening bouts for those involved. Yep it was most definitely time.

The world turned and me and dad got on with our lives even though someone was missing. We still loved boxing and went to all the big fights but it wasn't the same. Ali wasn't there.

By the time mid 1980 came along, I was married, had bought a house, had a large mortgage, had an Old English Sheepdog, came out of the Butchery trade and was working for the Post Office.

Dad had given up the fish stall and was working as a driver for Harvey's Curtains, where mum just happened to be the tea lady.

Life had changed dramatically for me and dad since Cassius Clay fought Henry Cooper all those years ago in 1963.

The Heavyweight division was being dominated by Larry Holmes. He was beating everyone and looked like the perfect heir to Ali's throne.

So it came as a bit of a shock when I was at work having a tea break and heard the news on the radio.

"Muhammad Ali is coming out of retirement to face Larry Holmes in October."

I couldn't wait for the day to end. I didn't go straight home to my wife that night. I went back to Mum and Dads. He looked at me as I walked in.

"I knew you'd be here. I told mum earlier. He'll be here."

Mum pushed a cup of tea in front of me, then left me and dad to talk boxing. I started.

"Why dad? Why does he want to come back? It's nonsense. Holmes is in his prime, he's almost ten years younger, he's quick and strong. He'll kill him."

Dad agreed.

"I don't think he can give it up son. He believes he's invincible."

We went to Gants Hill Cinema in Ilford on October 2nd 1980 to see Larry Holmes take on Muhammad Ali. Hoping for the impossible to happen, but deep down expecting the worse.

We watched in absolute horror as Holmes hit Ali with everything he had and hardly received a punch back in return. It was the most one sided fight I have ever seen. At first we thought he was doing his usual Rope a Dope, where he leaned back on the ropes and encouraged his opponent to hit him hoping to tire him out. But this was different. He just took more and more punishment. It was a miracle that he lasted as long as he did. His trainer Angelo Dundee finally called a halt to the fiasco in the eleventh round.

The actor Sylvester Stallone who was at ringside said "It was like watching an autopsy on a man who is still alive."

At the age of twenty-two, I sat in the cinema with my head in my hands and tears in my eyes. I couldn't look at dad in fear of breaking down.

It was most definitely the end of something really, really special.

Despite the battering, and the world praying him not to, Ali boxed on. He had one more fight fourteen months later against Trevor Berbick. It was the only fight me and dad didn't want to see, so we stayed away. Ali was beat in ten rounds. He never fought again.

Our hero died on the 3rd June 2016. He wasn't a saint as some would have us believe, but he was a great man. He stood up for his beliefs and proved to the world that if you try hard enough you can be anything you want to be. One thing is for sure he was "The Greatest" boxer the world has ever seen.

She Cut her Hair

Friday. 15.00pm

"Woke up this morning and just thought, hey why not?"

"Well I think you're very brave Sue. It looks great. When did you last have it cut?"

"2008. Just before I met Kenny."

There was an awkward silence between the two of them. Jackie wanted to say something about Kenny but decided it was best if she kept her thoughts to herself. Sue had once confided in her that Kenny had forbidden her to ever cut her hair.

"Well, as I said. It looks great. Short hair really suits you, AND, makes you look at least ten years younger!"

They both laughed.

Sue opened up a bottle of cheap white wine and poured them both a large glass. She handed one to Jackie and the two of them sat down at the kitchen table. They touched glasses.

"Cheers Sue. It's nice to catch up, haven't seen you for ages. So, apart from the new haircut, what's new?"

She was avoiding asking the obvious question, which was, "Where's Kenny?" The scumbag was usually lurking somewhere.

"Not much really. Works shit, but it's a job and I did get a nice bonus last month because the department did well."

"Great news. Spending it on something nice. Holiday perhaps?"

Sue put down her glass and smiled. In fact it was more than a smile. It was a full blown grin that made her cheeks puff up like a hamster storing its food.

"Sort of. But not for me. For Kenny."

Jackie's response was instant. She spat out a mouthful of wine all over the kitchen table.

"KENNY!"

"Yeh poor thing. He said he needed a break. You know, what with him being out of work for the past five years. He said it's been really stressful. So I gave him the money to go to Marbella with his mates for a week."

She looked at her watch.

"Should be getting on the plane right about now."

Six Hours Earlier.

"You packed my case yet Sue?"

"Just doing it now honey. Ready in a tick."

"Well fucking hurry up, the cab will be here in a few minutes."

Flushed, she stumbled down the stairs carrying a posh holdall and a much larger suitcase.

"All done."

Sue placed the bags by the front door and handed him a brown envelope.

"In here are your tickets and passport. When you get to the departure gate just give the man the envelope. Everything he needs is in there. "

"Yeh, yeh, yeh. Boring stuff, now what about the money?"

She gave him a large wad of notes.

"Here's two hundred in sterling and another six hundred in euros."

Kenny never said a word just took the envelope and put it in his pocket. He began to count the cash but was interrupted by the sound of a car horn from outside. He picked up his bags, opened the front door and headed down the path to the waiting taxi. With his back to her he shouted out.

"Don't forget to tape the football on Sunday!"

She waived him goodbye but he was far too busy putting his bags into the cab to notice. Seconds later he was gone.

She smiled, put on her coat and headed for the hairdressers.

Twenty Four Hours Earlier.

Sue was amazed at how much stuff there was on the internet. Google, Youtube, Wikipedia all had the information she was looking for. She printed off pages of diagrams, lists of equipment, chemicals needed and formulas required. A few of these pages she put into a brown envelope with the tickets and passport and the rest she slipped into a suitcase between two immaculately ironed shirts. Underneath these were the twelve "D" sized batteries placed neatly in two rows of six along with Kenny's old mobile phone that she'd found in the drawer of his bedside table. She went to the kitchen and took out a long ten inch carving knife and carefully wrapped a tea towel around it. This she placed at the bottom of a fake Louis Vuitton holdall.

She took out her mobile and dialled a number.

"Hi, I'd like to make an appointment for nine o'clock tomorrow morning please. Wash and cut."

She paused and then began to laugh.

"It might take some time. I haven't had it cut for seven years."

Thirty Six Hours Earlier.

"Sue, have you ironed my blue check shirt?"

"Yes babe, it's hanging in the wardrobe. I did it today."

A few minutes later Kenny appeared slapping after shave on his designer stubble cheeks. He held out his hand.

"Forty quid should do it. I'll need to buy a couple of rounds of drinks for the lads and then we might go for a curry."

Sue picked up her purse and took out two twenty pound notes. She handed them to Kenny.

"Better give us another tenner. Just in case."

She did as she was told and took out another ten pound note.

"Right I'm off. Don't wait up. Might be a late one."

She heard the door slam and breathed a sigh of relief. Now she could relax and watch whatever she wanted on TV. She heard a bell ring. The sound a mobile phone makes when a text or email comes through. Her phone was beside her. It wasn't hers.

The bell rang again. The sound was coming from underneath the kitchen table. She got on her hands and knees and saw Kenny's mobile on the floor. She picked it up. He'd be livid that he'd forgotten it. It would be her fault of course. It always was. She thought about taking it to the pub but Kenny was paranoid about his phone. She wasn't allowed to go anywhere near it. In fact this was the first time she'd ever touched it. The screen lit up and she could see that the text was from someone called Babs. It simply said "Can't wait." But she could also see the text above it. The text that Kenny had sent. She read it. "She's fallen for it babe. Stupid Cow. We're off to Marbella! See you at the airport. XXXXX."

Calmly she put the phone down on the table and sat down again in the chair. The door burst open. It was Kenny.

"You seen my phone? Can't find the bloody thing."

She composed herself.

"No I haven't seen it."

He saw it on the table. Walked over, picked it up and put it in his pocket. He walked back out without saying another word.

A full minute passed. She just stared into space. Then the shaking began, slowly at first, then faster and faster. She stood up, threw her head back and started to scream.

Forty Eight Hours Earlier.

"Look, all I'm saying is, it would do me good. Get the old batteries charged again. You know how stressed I've been since

I was made redundant all those years ago. I just can't seem to find a job and I hate relying on you for everything. So I thought that with that bit of bonus you got it would be best if I went off to Spain with the lads for a week. It'll be about a grand all in, and you did get twelve hundred quid Sue so there's a couple of hundred left for you. You could get a new dress or something."

There was one thing she wanted. One thing more than anything. Perhaps now was the time to bring it up.

"Okay honey. You go off to Spain with the boys. I agree it will do you good. But can I do something. Something just for me?"

"Of course you can. What do you want to do?"

Sue took a deep breath.

"Can I get my haircut? It's been seven years and it's always getting in the way. Can I? Please Kenny."

His face changed and he gave her "that look."

"Don't you fucking dare! Discussion over. I'm going. Now book the ticket and sort out the fucking euros and don't you ever talk about cutting your hair again."

The Keeper Of Secrets

Roger Fairbrass is dead. He died three days ago. Discovered in the armchair of his Mayfair flat by his housekeeper. He was 86. I only found out this morning by reading his obituary in the Telegraph. His full title was Sir Roger Fairbrass, CBE. I haven't seen Roger for a number of years and hopefully it was just old age that finally caught up with him.

I first met Roger in 1950 at Cambridge. He was a gifted student, far more self-assured and intelligent than me, but for some reason we hit it off immediately and became firm friends. If it wasn't for Roger I doubt if I would ever have passed my exams and obtained my degree. It was no surprise to anyone when he was recruited by the Foreign Office in 1953. I have no idea what he said to his superiors but thanks to Roger I joined him in the service in 1954.

Roger was a raconteur. Put him in a room full of strangers and he would have a crowd around him in minutes, hanging on his every word. He drank like a fish and smoked anything and everything that was possible. He quickly rose through the ranks and wherever he went he would always make sure there was a place for me.

The fifties and sixties were all about the war. Not a real war of course but the fake one. The cold war. We were men of secrets.

All kinds of secrets. Because of Roger we mixed in the company of the rich and famous. It wasn't uncommon to sit next to a member of royalty and chat about everything from fishing to sexual preferences. We became part of the elite. We were members of "Clubs" and "Societies".

Roger had an appetite for life. An appetite that had no limits. It was an appetite that was shared by many of his friends and at certain parties they would gorge themselves.

I am ashamed to say that I attended some of these parties and even took part in some of their ghoulish rituals. But please believe me, it was a different time, a different place, a different world back then.

Roger married in 1972. Her name was Shirley and she was the daughter of a well-known television presenter. It was all a sham of course. Roger needed to look presentable to the outside world. He needed someone to take to dinner parties, social events and royal functions. It didn't look natural for a man in his forties to attend on his own. Shirley was well aware of Roger's preferences and welcomed them, because she had certain sexual appetites of her own. On the outside they looked and acted like the perfect couple. But their lives were in fact completely separate. They shared the same house in Surrey, but it was so large that they only ever saw each other for social events. They both enjoyed a certain "lifestyle".

Roger held lavish parties at his Surrey home. They were by invitation only. Just six invitations were sent out. The people they were sent to were called "The Keepers Of Secrets." Each Keeper was allowed to bring three guests. The guests were carefully chosen and were sworn to secrecy. They were made very aware of the consequences if they discussed the party with anyone outside of the chosen few. Roger always organised the "Entertainment".

Once again I have to admit to being a "Keeper Of Secrets."

Once you were in that group of six it was impossible to get out. The risk to the others was just too great. The guest list at these events were household names. Stars of stage and screen. Current and ex Politicians and some even higher up the food chain.

He was rewarded for his loyalty (and silence) in 1989. He was knighted and became Sir Roger. Shirley was delighted of course, as this gave her the grand title of Lady Fairbrass. Unfortunately she died in 1994 after a long illness.

I last saw him at a garden party in 2006. He looked well and, as always, was surrounded by an entourage listening intently to his stories of daring do.

These past few years have been difficult for us "Keepers". Certain people have begun to look closely at what we did in those dark days when "anything" was possible. There was a time when those people would have been dealt with swiftly by our powerful friends. But not now. Things have changed. One by one "The Keepers" have been falling. Now Roger has gone, I am the last of the six still alive. I fear not for long.

So rather than wait for that visit that comes in the middle of the night. Or of a story that suddenly appears in one of the papers. I have decided that I will go of my own accord. I sit here with a glass of whisky and my old service revolver. Once my glass is empty then my days on this earth will end. This world has no place for "The Keepers Of Secrets" anymore. Perhaps it never did.

Goodbye.

The Granada Scorpio Mystery

"I have no idea what happened to him." That's the exact words I told the Police. "One day he was there and the next day he was gone."

There were lots of theories. But nothing conclusive. The police searched the whole of the estate and the surrounding area. House to house calls. But nothing. In 2002 the case was closed.

Jason Roberts was gone. God knows where and to be honest no one really cared. Especially the Police. They actually had a party at their local pub to celebrate.

He was a nasty piece of work was Jason. Mind like a switch. Say something wrong and he would turn...nasty. I once saw him cut an old man just because he commented on his new haircut.

Jason came in to the pub one day straight from the barbers. His hair was cut shorter than usual, and he looked like a convict. An old regular asked, in jest, if the council had done it. Jason turned and in a split second pulled a Stanley knife from his pocket and slashed the old man's face from his cheek to his mouth. No one said a word, they were too scared. So was I. I was just a kid back then.

Within a few years he ran the estate. Anything dodgy going down had to be run past him. He always wanted a cut of the proceeds of course, but if he gave the green light then you could do what you wanted. Drugs, armed robbery, stolen goods, Jason had his fingers in everything. No one crossed Jason, he was a volcano waiting to explode and when he did...well let's just say you wanted to be a million miles away.

Something came up. A big job. People were needed. People Jason knew and could trust. I was one of those young men.

I was promised £2000 for two hours work. It seemed like easy money to me. But then again the money was never really important.

I had to sit in a car and wait. Four men would arrive at exactly 3pm. From where I never knew. They would get in the car and I was to drive quickly, but within the law, all the way up to Birmingham. They would give my £2000 and then I'd leave the car somewhere and get a train home.

The timing was perfect. I got the car at 2.30 from a stranger. A nice big, jet black, Granada Scorpio. At 3pm they arrived looking pleased with themselves. Jason was one of them.

"Drive" was all he said.

I took the A1 through London and then the M1 up to the M6 and then straight to Birmingham. I dropped one of the men off at Walsall and the other two at Solihull. That just left me and Jason.

"Right, Change of plan, let's go home. Drop me at Woodford. There's a club there where the owner will swear I was there all day. Then take the car somewhere and torch it."

He laughed as he said it and passed me a Marks and Spencer carrier bag.

"There's two grand in there. Don't spunk it all at once."

He leaned back in his chair and fell asleep.

The car was never found and neither was Jason. The only person that turned up at the Woodford club that night was me. With a lot more than £2000.

I now run the estate. Oh and did I mention...that old boy that Jason cut? He was my dad.

The Couple From The Banjo

Ted and Florence Carter lived down the Banjo. Yep, that's where they lived. Down the Banjo. Now some of you won't know what a Banjo is. Let me explain.

When this particular council estate was being built back in the twenties, the architects decided to be a bit clever. Street designs included cul-de-sacs that were built in a particular shape. A long open walkway with a grass verge on either side suddenly opened up into a large circle of houses. They called it a Banjo because that's exactly what it looked like from above.

Ted and Florrie considered themselves lucky. They'd moved from a one bedroom flat in Bermondsey, South London to a three bedroom council house in the leafy suburbs of Dagenham. Here they survived the war, raised their five children, danced their way through the fifties, saw all of their children married in the sixties, cried with grief when they buried one of their sons, but cried with joy as they saw eleven grandchildren born in the seventies. It was now 1984.

They'd both been retired for a number of years and had settled into a daily routine. Everyone knew them as "that nice old couple who live down the banjo."

Ted's day was always the same. He was an early riser. At six thirty he was up, washed and shaved and taking Florrie up a nice cup of tea. Then he would walk the short distance to the paper shop where he would buy the Daily Mirror and the Sporting Life. Back indoors Florrie would serve up his breakfast of eggs and bacon at seven thirty which was washed down with two big mugs of tea. Florrie made the best tea in Dagenham. After which he would start to pick out his horses. One pound a day was his maximum bet. Yet he would pick out as many as eight horses and do them in doubles and trebles all for a few pence each. Then he'd tackle the crossword. He set himself a target of finishing it before ten o'clock. He rarely did. At ten thirty he changed into a suit with shirt and tie. He liked to look smart. He left the house and made his way to the betting shop to put on his bets. By midday he was walking through the doors of his local, The Royal Oak to have his "constitution."

His "constitution" was to stay there for two hours and have five or six pints of bitter. He met his pals here, played crib or dominoes and generally had a laugh. He was always indoors by three at the very latest. Time for a quick nap till four thirty and ready for Florrie's delicious dinner at half past five. The old Victorian piano in the front room had also survived the decades just as they had and usually took a bashing from Ted at around seven for an hour. They'd both sit down to watch a bit of television for a while in the evening and then off to bed at ten.

Florrie's day was slightly different.

Ted brought her up a cup of tea at six thirty. She would have preferred another hour's sleep but when Ted was up everyone else had to be awake as well. She was also convinced that the tea was to make sure she was awake and ready to start cooking his fry up. He insisted on having his breakfast on the table at seven thirty, so she started cooking his bacon and eggs at seven fifteen. The look on his face was pure evil if god- forbid she put the plate in front of him at seven thirty five! She watched as he gambled away seven pounds a week. Money that could be better spent on house-keeping. Ted was in charge of their combined pensions and gave her what he thought she could manage the household bills with. The rest he spent on himself. Either gambling or alcohol. Besides, he never won. If he did he kept it quiet, she never saw any of his winnings. Her favourite time was when he left the house at eleven and didn't return until three. She would sit and have tea and biscuits and watch a bit of daytime television. But not for long. There was a bed to make, suits to press, shirts to iron, washing up to do, hoover and duster to put round and of course she had to start cooking the evening meal. Ted liked the house to be spotless. Even though he'd never picked up a duster in his life. According to him that was her job. He also liked a proper cooked meal every night. Meat, potatoes, veg, gravy and a nice pudding to follow. So most afternoons were spent baking meat pies, meat puddings, jam sponges or ginger cakes. When Ted came home at three, usually a bit worse for wear, he would sit down in the armchair and fall asleep. He would then snore for the next two hours. After that the piano would feel the full force of his massive fingers as he bashed away at various notes to try to get a tune out of the old Joanna. He would sit at the dining room table at five twenty five, knife and fork in hand waiting impatiently to be fed. She would put the dinner in front of him and he would start to eat. He never said thank you. He turned on the television after dinner and HE would choose what they watched until they went to bed. She was never allowed to stay up after ten o'clock.

It was Wednesday and it was after four. Ted was late home from the pub. She was in the middle of making bread pudding in the kitchen and worrying just how drunk Ted might be when he eventually got home. What mood would he be in? Would he raise his hands or simply fall asleep in the chair? She heard a key unlock the front door.

She left the kitchen and went into the hallway. Standing there were all her grown up children. Kay, the eldest spoke quietly.

"Mum, come and sit down, we've got something to tell you."

Kay took her mums hand and led her into the front room. She sat her down in Ted's armchair. They all took their places on the sofa. Kay knelt down beside the armchair.

"Mum, it's about dad. He felt a bit unwell in the pub today and they called for an ambulance. One of the other regulars called me at home. He had a heart attack mum. He's gone. Dad's gone."

Kay squeezed her mums hand and started to cry. Florrie put her head in her hands and started to rock back and forth.

"It's okay mum, we're all here for you. It's going to be okay."

Florrie took her hands away from her face. She was smiling. She started to laugh. Uncontrollably.

Kay looked at the others who were all bemused by their mum's reaction.

"It's okay, someone go and put the kettle on. It's shock. Mum's just in shock!"

That Morning

I got up late that morning, too late. My head was pounding like cannon balls being fired from an old galleon ship. Far too much whiskey was drunk the night before and far too much money was lost on that bloody poker game. The last hand could have been mine if it wasn't for DAVE. I had two pairs, Aces and Queens. I was confident I'd take the pot. But DAVE with his fucking full house did me like a kipper. Over three grand in the pot and DAVE took the lot. Although Dave was my best mate, that morning I hated Dave. That morning Dave was most definitely a wanker!

But, that morning I decided to be positive. The dawn brought with it new possibilities. The papers arrived and The Racing Post would surely be my saviour. After an hour's studying I had the day planned. Romford Dog Track would be the place to get my money back and a few extra quid on top. I got there at eleven o'clock, just in time for the first race. I didn't bet in that race, just watched. Trap two, the favourite, led all the way and won by a distance. I remembered the words of my late Uncle Mick. "If the favourite wins the first, back it in the next six races." Unfortunately Uncle Mick died young and broke. But today that didn't matter. Today was a favourite day!

I ordered a pint and wandered around the track hoping to see some familiar faces. I was looking for Old Charlie. He had dogs, half a dozen at least. He knew what he was talking about. If Old Charlie gave you a tip, you lumped on. Once, he gave me a tip for a dog at Catford. It pissed home at seven to one. I had five hundred quid on it and went home with over four grand that day. Yep, I needed to see Old Charlie.

That first beer was hard to get down, but the second was smooth, hit the spot. A whisky chaser helped it on its way. I was beginning to feel human again and the headache quickly became a distant memory. I checked what cash I had in my pocket. Six hundred and twenty quid. But I also had my emergency card. A card I'd never used. A card that would allow me to draw out up to a maximum of five hundred quid if I needed it. I was deciding whether or not to go to the cash machine when I spotted Randy Roger at the bar. He was with a gorgeous bird, at least ten years younger than him and with the best pair of tits I'd seen in a long time. Randy Roger was punching well above his weight these days. I wandered over.

"Hi Rog, any luck?

He had that smarmy grin on his face, he knew what I was thinking. Just to rub it in he kissed his dolly bird on the cheek and grabbed her arse at the same time. She giggled like a naughty schoolgirl. He turned, looked at me and winked.

"Get on the four dog in the next race. Mate of mine owns it. Says it can't be beat."

I walked away a happy man. Good old Randy Roger.

I put my bet on. Three hundred quid on trap four. The bell rang, the lights went down and the traps opened. The four dog came out last and that's exactly where he finished. LAST.

I looked for Randy Roger and his tart. They were nowhere to be seen. Why did I listen to that pratt? The only thing he knew about dogs was how to shag them!

I noticed one of the local trainers, Tony Cook, at the bar. He was talking to a very smart and rather ferocious looking man. I wandered over and stood next to them trying to overhear their conversation. I caught a few words.

"Look your dog will win, most definitely. It's fit, fitter than it's ever been. I expect it to win by a large margin."

That was good enough for me. I looked through the programme. Tony Cook had only one dog in the next race. Trap Three. It was six to one. I put three hundred quid on it. I watched as it came out of the traps like a fucking flying machine. It was four lengths in front at the first bend. I raised my arms in triumph expecting it to go clear and win comfortably. But it didn't. It tired. It was as if there was a sniper in the crowd that shot the fucker at the final bend. Every dog passed it and it finished stone last. I caught sight of poor old Tony Cook being dragged into the men's toilets by the scruff of his neck by a very disgruntled owner.

I was desperate. I needed a winner and fast. But that morning my luck was about to change. I spotted Old Charlie talking to a couple of blokes I'd never seen before. They were all huddled together. Lots of nods, winks and whispers going on. This looked promising. I waited a few minutes until they parted company. The two big strangers walked off and left Old Charlie on his own. I called over.

"Charlie. How you doing mate?"

Old Charlie came over. I was sure the man was worth a fortune, yet he dressed like a tramp and drove an old Volvo estate car. He didn't answer my question. Just leaned into me and whispered in my ear.

"Those two guys I was just talking to have brought a young dog over from Ireland. It's running in the next race. Trap three.

Apparently over there it's beating everything in sight. Some kind of super dog. Get on it!"

Old Charlie walked away. I loved that man. True gent.

I had five minutes before the start of the race. Time for another quick beer and a nice chaser. I went over and spoke to the spotty faced kid behind the bar.

"Pint of Stella please mate and a large Glenfiddich."

He quickly served up the drinks and I paid with my last twenty pound note. I drank down the Scotch and took a swig of the Lager. Time to use the emergency card and get my five hundred quid. I walked over to the cash machine. I pushed the card into the slot. And THAT was the morning.

THAT was the morning...I forgot my PIN number.

Billy Greaves Secret

My best friend Billy Greaves wasn't the sharpest tool in the box. People used to joke that his shoes had "L" and "R" written on them, just in case he got confused.

Neither did he have the looks of David Beckham. Some would say he had a face that only a mother could love.

He was short, about five feet six inches tall. Scrawny, weighing only about nine stone. His day job was as a porter at the local fish market and he ALWAYS smelt of fish.

To be fair he always tried to better himself by taking various evening classes but as far as I knew they didn't come to much.

So it came as a big surprise to everyone, especially me, when he started dating Wendy Hiller. The most beautiful girl in town.

Wendy had everything. A perfect body and the face of an angel. She was witty and charming and had been going out with Big Jim Sanders, the captain of the local rugby team. But for some crazy reason that no one could figure out, she dumped him for Billy Greaves.

People started making jokes like "Well maybe he has something we don't know about" or "Maybe he has hidden talents" all said with a nudge and a wink. But I can assure you after spending time with Billy in the showers after football training he wasn't blessed with anything special in the "downstairs" department.

Wendy was absolutely besotted with him. If you saw them together she always had that dreamy look in her eyes and hung on his every word. It was rumoured that she phoned him at least six times a day just to hear his voice and tell him how much she loved him.

Wendy came from a wealthy family who owned the biggest house in the best street in town. They also adored Billy. Her Dad had several builders merchants in the area and was our local Councillor. Some even thought that one day he would be our MP. It wasn't long after Wendy introduced her parents to Billy that they welcomed into their fabulous home and even bought him a brand new sports car.

After a whirlwind romance and quick engagement, they were to be married. It was a special day and all friends and family were invited. I was the Best Man. After the ceremony we all sat down to a three course meal. All fish of course, fresh from the market. Whitebait to start, followed by Monkfish as the main course and then anchovie ice cream for dessert.

During the evenings celebrations a man arrived that no one except Billy seemed to recognise. I've known Billy for over twenty years and I'd never seen this man before.

Billy rushed over and greeted him with a big man hug. They stood talking at the bar for ages and finally Billy went off to have the first dance with his new wife.

As the DJ begun to play "Just the way you are" by Billy Joel, we all watched as Wendy put her head on Billy's shoulder and they smooched slowly to the music. I heard one of the bridesmaids say to her friend "Ah look he's whispering in her ear. Probably telling her how much he loves her."

While the music was playing I decided to find out who the stranger was. I walked over and stood beside him at the bar. I offered him my hand to shake. He did.

"Hello there. I'm Steve. Billy's Best Man"

The stranger smiled back at me.

"Pleasure to meet you Steve. My name is Robert. Robert Johnson."

I was anxious to find out more.

"So how do you know Billy?"

The man took a sip of his drink and continued.

"I met him a couple of years ago. He attended my evening classes. In fact he was my star pupil. Never seen anyone pick up the skills as quickly as Billy.

I was intrigued. I'd known Billy had tried everything from carpentry to psychology but never knew he was actually good at any on them.

"Really, what subject?"

The man looked at me and grinned.

"Hypnotism. He's the best I've seen in a long time."

Terry Palmer

There's a neon sign above the Pharmacy across the street. It's flashing the number thirty- two. That's the temperature. Even though I'm sitting in the shade with an ice cold beer in my hand I can feel the sweat running down my cheek.

What am I doing here? In a small town in Southern Spain? All alone and 1500 miles from home?

Two words. Terry Palmer.

Let me tell you about Terry. We were mates. No, that's not even close. We were BEST mates. Terry was like a brother to me.

We met thirty- five years ago at the age of eleven. First day of senior school and everyone was nervous. Some older boys started picking on Terry. I was always a big lad for my age and stepped in to help. I pushed one of the boys hard and he fell to the ground, I stood over him with my foot on his chest. The other kid ran off. No one picked on Terry from that day onwards.

For some strange reason we just clicked, even though we were so different. Terry was a bright kid, always top of the class. Me?

I was into Sport. Didn't matter what it was, I wanted to be the best at it. I played Rugby, Football and Cricket. I had trials for most London football clubs but never quite made the grade. At sixteen I left school and went to work for my Uncle's demolition company. Terry stayed on to get his "A" Levels.

At nineteen I was earning good money and renting my own flat. My money was spent on beer and birds. Terry went to Bristol University to study something called Quantum Physics.

Although we were miles apart we still kept in touch. I would spend a week or two at his campus sleeping on the floor of his tiny room. When he had term breaks he would come and stay with me. I was earning and he wasn't so I paid for everything. We even went to Benidorm for two weeks, but to be honest I can't remember much about it. I think we might have been a bit drunk while we were there.

At twenty- two Terry got his degree and went to work for a company called QMC. They were big in Hi-Tec security equipment. I was still with the demolition company but was now running my own small crew.

Over the next few years me and Terry would meet twice a week after work for a beer or three. As much as I loved him there were two things about him that drove me mad. He always wore the same bloody aftershave. Fahrenheit! It had a strong distinct smell that I just found overpowering. He also did something bizarre with a crisp packet. He would order the beers and two bags of crisps. When he'd finished his bag he would very slowly and precisely fold it up and tie it into a knot. He would wait for me to finish mine and then do the same. For some reason it drove me nuts!

I met Caroline in 1995, when I was twenty- six. We were married two years later. Terry of course was my best man. He met Sandra in 1998 and married her within six months. And yes, of course, I was his best man. Carol and Sandra became good friends and that made it easy for me and Terry to spend time together. We had season tickets for our beloved West Ham United and went to every game, home and away.

Caroline and I never had kids. We tried for a while but nothing seemed to happen and we just sort of accepted it. Terry and Sandra had two in the space of four years. Boy and a girl. Great kids. Me and Caroline were god parents to both.

Terry died six years ago in 2009. He was forty years old.

No one was really sure what happened. His car went out of control on the way to work. It hit a tree and burst into flames. He could only be identified by his personal belonging. His watch, wedding ring and a St Christopher that he always wore around his neck.

An inquest decided that he must have had a heart attack whilst driving. We all prayed that he died before the car caught fire.

Things haven't been the same since Terry passed. Caroline says that I've become distant. To be honest I miss him so much that sometimes I find it difficult to talk. This can go on for days. My Doctor calls them "Episodes". I dream about Terry every night, vivid dreams that make me convinced that he's not really dead. It's as if he wants me to find him. I've told Caroline but she dismisses it and then checks that I've taken my medication.

Anyway, that gives you some idea of how close me and Terry were. But it still doesn't explain why I'm here in Coin just a few miles away from Mijas in Southern Spain.

Caroline thought we needed a break so she booked us a two-week holiday on the Costa Del Sol. Luxury 5 Star Hotel to cater for our every need. "Quality Time" she called it.

Well, after four days of "Quality Time", just laying by the pool and drinking countless gin and tonics. I was bored. So this morning I decided to hire a car and explore some of the local towns. Caroline didn't want to come but said it would be good for me to have a day on my own.

I drove through Mijas and up into the hills. I saw a sign for Coin and decided that as my stomach had started to think my throat had been cut, it might be wise to get a bit of lunch and a cold beer.

The town was quiet. No surprise really. It was Siesta time. People were either at home having lunch or an afternoon nap.

I parked the car outside the Pharmacy. Opposite was a small traditional looking Spanish bar. There was a man outside sitting at one of the tables. He was wearing a panama hat, head down and reading a newspaper. As I looked over he raised his head to take a swig of his bottled beer. I couldn't believe what I was seeing. It couldn't be him. It just couldn't.

He saw me. Quickly put down his beer and went inside.

I got out of the car, ran across the road and into the bar. Apart from a dark haired man behind the counter. It was empty. I shouted at him.

"The man. The man. Where is he?"

He pointed to a door at the other end of the bar. It was partly open and light was flooding in from the street. I ran to the door and into the blazing heat. The street was empty.

I shouted again.

"Terry. Terry!"

There was no answer. The only sound was a dog barking from a local balcony. I wandered up and down the street for at least twenty minutes before I finally gave up and re-entered the bar. I ordered a beer. This time I spoke slowly and quietly to the barman.

"The man who was just here. Do you know him. Know where he lives?"

His English wasn't great. He shook his head.

"No sir. Stranger. Stranger."

I nodded, went back out and sat at the same table as the man I thought was my dead friend. And that's when I saw it. Just there on the marble table.

A crisp packet tied carefully into a knot.

So now you know why I'm here. Sitting in a small Spanish town 1500 miles from home, holding a tied up crisp packet and the faint smell of Fahrenheit disturbing my nostrils.

And now I can't go home. Not until I find out what the fuck is going on...

My mind is racing. I'm on my fourth beer. I look at my watch. It's ten past three. The watch always reminds me of Terry. Same make and model as his. Omega Speedmaster.

The whole thing seems unreal. But I know I saw him. I just know it. So if he's out there somewhere I have to find him. But where do I start?

I should call Caroline. I dial her number.

"Hi babe. I've got a slight problem. I'm in the middle of nowhere up in the mountains and the bloody car has broken down. I've called the car hire people and they say someone is coming out to have a look at it but you know what Spain is like. Manjana. Manjana."

She sounds concerned.

"You okay?"

"Yeh fine. Just got to wait for the breakdown people and I'll be back."

"That's not what I mean. Are you OKAY?"

"Yeh, really. I'm fine. Don't worry. Look I've got to go. I'll call you a bit later."

I hang up. I feel guilty for lying but what else can I do. Say I've just seen my dead best friend? Don't think so.

I walk back into the bar. It's still empty but for the man behind the bar. I smile at him and speak slowly.

"So. The man... who was just here. He is a... Stranger?"

He shrugs his shoulders.

"Yes Sir. A stranger. I no see him before today."

I try not to laugh. He sounds like Manuel from Fawlty Towers. I pay for my drinks and leave.

I'm standing outside and wondering where to go next. The Pharmacy seems like the logical place to go. Somewhere in there someone must speak English. I look up at the neon sign. It's showing thirty – five degrees.

Inside it's cool, the air conditioning is working well. A young, attractive, olive skinned lady smiles and says "Hola."

"Do you speak English?"

Her smile widens, exposing a large amount of gleaming white teeth.

"Yes, but it is not very good."

I smile back.

"Better than my Spanish. That's for sure. Is there a Hotel in town, or a place to stay?"

She shakes her head.

"No Hotel. But...there are rooms at El Caliente. Is just a few minutes' walk."

She points in the direction of the main road heading out of town. I'm guessing it's a kind of guest house.

I thank her and begin to leave but something catches my eye. Something familiar in a glass cabinet on the wall. There amongst a dozen or so bottles of aftershave is a small red object that I recognise. Fahrenheit.

I point to the bottle.

"How much?"

"Is forty euros.".

For some reason I feel obliged to buy the aftershave. So I hand over forty euros and leave. I walk along the road that leads out of town and find El Caliente after ten minutes. It's as I expected. A small guest house.

Inside it's full of dark wooden furniture. The whole reception area looks dingy, probably because all the windows are covered with shutters to keep the place cool. There's a bell on the counter. I ring it. A man appears almost out of nowhere. He doesn't say anything. Just kind of gestures for me to speak.

"You have rooms? A spare room for one night?"

He nods. I think he says something but can't be sure. He opens up a book that's in front of him on the counter. Now he speaks. I'm surprised at how good his English is.

"You sign the book. Name and where you live. Then you pay me thirty euros for one night. Breakfast is extra five euros."

He spins the book round and pushes it towards me. I quickly look at the other names in the book. One name jumps out at me. Thomas Porter. Could it be? TP. Same initials as Terry Palmer.

I point to the name.

"This man. He is staying here?"

Once again he nods.

"Yes. He is a friend of yours?"

Now I'm excited.

"Yes. Yes. Is he here now?"

"No. He went out this morning. No return yet."

I pay the thirty euros and take a key for room nine. But I don't want to leave the reception area in case he comes back and I miss him.

"Can I wait here in reception. I want to surprise him when he returns."

The man just shrugs his shoulders.

"Okay. You want drink. Beer, Brandy?"

"Cold beer would be great. Thank you."

I sit down on a hard wooden chair and notice something in an ashtray on the table in front of me.

It's there. Another tied up crisp packet.

He's here, he's definitely here. My mobile rings. It's Caroline. I ignore it. Not now. Not now. I notice she's rung seven times since I spoke to her and left voice messages. I can't speak to her. I just have to see Terry and find out what's going on.

The Spanish man brings me 2 bottles of San Miguel and one glass. I thank him and pour the first. It slides down easily and now I'm on to the second. I fiddle with the St Christopher hanging round my neck. All I can think about is Terry.

He must be in some big trouble. He's running away from something. Something that's out of his control. Something he's scared of. But I'm here. As always ready to help. Ready to protect him from the bad guys.

And then it happens. I see him. He walks into reception and stands there looking straight at me.

"You shouldn't be here."

I want to hug him. It's been six years since I saw him yet he looks exactly the same. He's even wearing the clothes that he wore on the last day I saw him. Jeans, blue T- shirt and white trainers and that stupid hat that he always wore in the summer. Even though I told him he looked like a complete prat.

He sits down opposite me and shakes his head. He says the words again.

"You shouldn't be here."

For some reason I can't speak or move. I want to answer him but nothing works. His expression changes.

"Go home to Caroline. She'll be worried."

The Spanish hotel owner looks across at me. He looks concerned.

"Senor? You okay?"

I just look over at him. I still can't speak. I hear Terry's voice again. He speaks softly this time.

"Look at you. You wear the same watch and St Christopher that I used to wear. You buy a bottle of Fahrenheit every time you go out. Now you've even started tying up crisp packets, just like I used to do. It wasn't your fault, you couldn't always be there to protect me. Let me go mate. Please...just let me go."

He stands up, smiles at me, turns and walks away. Just as he gets to the door he turns to face me again. This time his smile turns into a wide grin.

"Besides, you've got someone else to protect now mate. Ask Caroline."

And then he was gone. I hear the voice of the Hotel owner again.

"Senor, senor. You okay?"

I suddenly feel fit and well again, the first time I've felt this way in years. I stand up and walk over to the reception desk. I take off my watch and St Christopher and place them along with the bottle of Fahrenheit on the counter. I smile at the nervous looking Spaniard.

"These are for you. I don't need them anymore."

I walk along the main road towards the car. My mobile vibrates in my pocket. It's Caroline.

I answer it and before she has a chance to speak, the words tumble from my mouth.

"You're pregnant, aren't you?"

There's a pause before she answers.

"How did you know?"

I'm now running to the car. I can't wait to get home.

"It doesn't matter babe. I'm coming home. It's over."

Find out more about the author, Joe Lawrence.

His first book on Amazon

http://www.amazon.co.uk/s/ref=nb_sb_ss_i_0_21?url=search-alias%3Daps&fie...

Author Interviews.

.http://spitalfieldslife.com/2015/03/22/joe-lawrence-traditional-butcher-...

https://authorsinterviews.wordpress.com/2016/08/22/here-is-my-interview-...

Printed in Great Britain
by Amazon

84974882R00099